95806

3A/20

THE LOVER

MARGUERITE DURAS

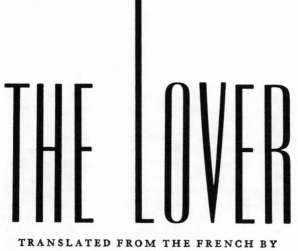

THE LOVER

TRANSLATED FROM THE FRENCH BY
BARBARA BRAY

PANTHEON BOOKS, NEW YORK

All rights reserved under International and Pan-American Copy-
right Conventions. Published in the United States by Pantheon
Books, a division of Random House, Inc., New York, and simul-
taneously in Canada by Random House of Canada Limited,
Toronto. Originally published in France as *L'Amant* by Les Edi-
tions de Minuit. Copyright © 1984 by Les Editions de Minuit.
This translation published in Great Britain by William Collins
Sons & Co. Ltd., London.

Library of Congress Cataloging in Publication Data

Duras, Marguerite.
The lover.
Translation of: L'amant.
I. Title.
PQ2607.U8245A62613 1985   843'.912   84-26321
ISBN 0-394-54588-5

Book design by Gina Davis

MANUFACTURED IN THE UNITED STATES OF AMERICA

First American Edition

FOR BRUNO NUYTTEN

THE LOVER

One day, I was already old, in the entrance of a public place a man came up to me. He introduced himself and said, "I've known you for years. Everyone says you were beautiful when you were young, but I want to tell you I think you're more beautiful now than then. Rather than your face as a young woman, I prefer your face as it is now. Ravaged."

I often think of the image only I can see now, and of which I've never spoken. It's always there, in the same silence, amazing. It's the only image of myself I like, the only one in which I recognize myself, in which I delight.

Very early in my life it was too late. It was already too late when I was eighteen. Between eighteen and twenty-five my face took off in a new direction. I grew old at eighteen. I don't know if it's the same for everyone, I've never asked. But I believe I've heard of the way time can suddenly accelerate on people when they're going through even the most youthful and highly esteemed stages of life. My ageing was very sudden. I saw it spread over my features one by one, changing the relationship between them, making the eyes larger, the expression sadder, the mouth more final, leaving great creases in the forehead. But instead of being dismayed I watched this process with the same sort of interest I might have taken in the reading of a book. And I knew I was right, that one day it would slow down and take its normal course. The people who knew me at seventeen, when I went to France, were surprised when they saw me again two years later, at nineteen. And I've kept it ever since, the new face I had then. It has been my face. It's got older still, of course, but less, comparatively, than it would otherwise have done. It's scored with deep, dry wrinkles, the skin is cracked. But my face hasn't collapsed, as some with fine features have done. It's kept the same contours, but its substance has been laid waste. I have a face laid waste.

So, I'm fifteen and a half.

It's on a ferry crossing the Mekong River.

The image lasts all the way across.

I'm fifteen and a half, there are no seasons in that part of the world, we have just the one season, hot, monotonous, we're in the long hot girdle of the earth, with no spring, no renewal.

I'm at a state boarding school in Saigon. I eat and sleep there, but I go to classes at the French high school. My mother is a teacher and wants her girl to have a secondary education. "You have to go to high school." What was enough for her is not enough for her daughter. High school and then a good degree in mathematics. That was what had been dinned into me ever since I started school. It never crossed my mind I might escape the mathematics degree, I was glad to give her that hope. Every day I saw her planning her own and her children's future. There came a time when she couldn't plan anything very grand for her sons any more, so she planned other futures, makeshift ones, but they too served their purpose, they blocked in the time that lay ahead. I remember my younger brother's courses in bookkeeping. From the Universal Correspondence School—every year, every level. You have to catch up, my mother used to say. It would last for three days, never four. Never. We'd drop the Universal School whenever my mother was posted to another place. And begin again in the next. My mother kept it up for ten years. It wasn't any good. My younger brother became an accountant's clerk in Saigon. There was no technical school in the colonies; we owed my elder brother's departure for France to that. He stayed in France for several years to study at the technical school. But he didn't keep it up. My mother must have known. But she had no choice, he had to be got away from the other two children. For several years he was no longer part of the family. It was while he was away that my mother bought the land. A terrible business, but for us, the children who were left, not so terrible as the presence of the killer would have been, the child-killer of the night, of the night of the hunter.

I've often been told it was because of spending all one's childhood in too strong a sun. But I've never believed it. I've also been told it was because being poor made us brood. But no, that wasn't it. Children like little old men because of chronic hunger, yes. But us, no, we weren't hungry. We were white children, we were ashamed, we sold our furniture, but we weren't hungry, we had a houseboy and we ate. Sometimes, admittedly, we ate garbage—storks, baby crocodiles—but the garbage was cooked and served by a houseboy, and sometimes we refused it, too, we indulged in the luxury of declining to eat. No, something occurred when I was eighteen to make this face happen. It must have been at night. I was afraid of myself, afraid of God. In the daylight I was less afraid, and death seemed less important. But it haunted me all the time. I wanted to kill—my elder brother, I wanted to kill him, to get the better of him for once, just once, and see him die. I wanted to do it to remove from my mother's sight the object of her love, that son of hers, to punish her for loving him so much, so badly, and above all—as I told myself, too—to save my younger brother, my younger brother, my child, save him from the living life of that elder brother superimposed on his own, from that black veil over the light, from the law which was decreed and represented by the elder brother, a human being, and yet which was an animal law, filling every moment of every day of the younger brother's life with fear, a fear that one day reached his heart and killed him.

I've written a good deal about the members of my family, but then they were still alive, my mother and my brothers. And I skirted around them, skirted around all these things without really tackling them.

.   .   .

The story of my life doesn't exist. Does not exist. There's never any center to it. No path, no line. There are great spaces where you pretend there used to be someone, but it's not true, there was no one. The story of one small part of my youth I've already written, more or less—I mean, enough to give a glimpse of it. Of this part, I mean, the part about the crossing of the river. What I'm doing now is both different and the same. Before, I spoke of clear periods, those on which the light fell. Now I'm talking about the hidden stretches of that same youth, of certain facts, feelings, events that I buried. I started to write in surroundings that drove me to reticence. Writing, for those people, was still something moral. Nowadays it often seems writing is nothing at all. Sometimes I realize that if writing isn't, all things, all contraries confounded, a quest for vanity and void, it's nothing. That if it's not, each time, all things confounded into one through some inexpressible essence, then writing is nothing but advertisement. But usually I have no opinion, I can see that all options are open now, that there seem to be no more barriers, that writing seems at a loss for somewhere to hide, to be written, to be read. That its basic unseemliness is no longer accepted. But at that point I stop thinking about it.

Now I see that when I was very young, eighteen, fifteen, I already had a face that foretold the one I acquired through drink in middle age. Drink accomplished what God did not. It also served to kill me; to kill. I acquired that drinker's face before I drank. Drink only confirmed it. The space for it existed in me. I knew it the same as other people, but, strangely, in advance. Just as the space existed in me for desire. At the age of fifteen I had the face of pleasure, and yet I had no knowledge of pleasure. There was no mistaking that face. Even my mother must have seen it. My brothers did. That was how everything started for me— with that flagrant, exhausted face, those rings around the eyes, in advance of time and experience.

I'm fifteen and a half. Crossing the river. Going back to Saigon I feel I'm going on a journey, especially when I take the bus, and this morning I've taken the bus from Sadec, where my mother is the headmistress of the girls' school. It's the end of some school vacation, I forget which. I've spent it in the little house provided with my mother's job. And today I'm going back to Saigon, to the boarding school. The native bus left from the marketplace in Sadec. As usual my mother came to see me off, and put me in the care of the driver. She always puts me in the care of the Saigon bus drivers, in case there's an accident, or a fire, or a rape, or an attack by pirates, or a fatal mishap on the ferry. As usual the driver had me sit near him in the front, in the section reserved for white passengers.

. . .

I think it was during this journey that the image became detached, removed from all the rest. It might
have existed, a photograph might have been taken, just
like any other, somewhere else, in other circumstances.
But it wasn't. The subject was too slight. Who would
have thought of such a thing? The photograph could
only have been taken if someone could have known
in advance how important it was to be in my life, that
event, that crossing of the river. But while it was hap-
pening, no one even knew of its existence. Except God.
And that's why—it couldn't have been otherwise—the
image doesn't exist. It was omitted. Forgotten. It never
was detached or removed from all the rest. And it's to
this, this failure to have been created, that the image
owes its virtue: the virtue of representing, of being the
creator of, an absolute.

So it's during the crossing of a branch of the Mekong,
on the ferry that plies between Vinh Long and Sadec
in the great plain of mud and rice in southern Cochin
China. The Plain of the Birds.

I get off the bus. I go over to the rails. I look at the
river. My mother sometimes tells me that never in my
whole life shall I ever again see rivers as beautiful and
big and wild as these, the Mekong and its tributaries

going down to the sea, the great regions of water soon to disappear into the caves of ocean. In the surrounding flatness stretching as far as the eye can see, the rivers flow as fast as if the earth sloped downward.

I always get off the bus when we reach the ferry, even at night, because I'm always afraid, afraid the cables might break and we might be swept out to sea. In the terrible current I watch my last moments. The current is so strong it could carry everything away—rocks, a cathedral, a city. There's a storm blowing inside the water. A wind raging.

I'm wearing a dress of real silk, but it's threadbare, almost transparent. It used to belong to my mother. One day she decided the color was too light for her and she gave it to me. It's a sleeveless dress with a very low neck. It's the sepia color real silk takes on with wear. It's a dress I remember. I think it suits me. I'm wearing a leather belt with it, perhaps a belt belonging to one of my brothers. I can't remember the shoes I used to wear in those days, only certain dresses. Most of the time I wore canvas sandals, no stockings. I'm speaking of the time before the high school in Saigon. Since then, of course, I've always worn shoes. This particular day I must be wearing the famous pair of gold lamé high heels. I can't see any others I could have been wearing, so I'm wearing them. Bargains, final reductions bought for me by my mother. I'm wearing these gold lamé shoes to school. Going to school in evening shoes decorated with little *diamanté* flowers. I insist on wearing them. I don't like myself in any others, and to this day I still like myself in them. These high heels are the first in my life, they're beautiful, they've eclipsed all the shoes that went before, the flat ones, for playing and running about, made of white canvas.

It's not the shoes, though, that make the girl look so strangely, so weirdly dressed. No, it's the fact that she's wearing a man's flat-brimmed hat, a brownish-pink fedora with a broad black ribbon.

The crucial ambiguity of the image lies in the hat.

How I came by it I've forgotten. I can't think who could have given it to me. It must have been my mother who bought it for me because I asked her. The one thing certain is that it was another markdown, another final reduction. But why was it bought? No woman, no girl wore a man's fedora in that colony then. No native woman, either. What must have happened is: I try it on just for fun, look at myself in the shop-keeper's glass, and see that there, beneath the man's hat, the thin awkward shape, the inadequacy of child-hood, has turned into something else. Has ceased to be a harsh, inescapable imposition of nature. Has become, on the contrary, a provoking choice of nature, a choice of the mind. Suddenly it's deliberate. Suddenly I see myself as another, as another would be seen, outside myself, available to all, available to all eyes, in circulation for cities, journeys, desire. I take the hat, and am never parted from it. Having got it, this hat that all by itself makes me whole, I wear it all the time. With the shoes it must have been much the same, but after the hat. They contradict the hat, as the hat contradicts the puny body, so they're right for me. I wear them all the time too, go overywhere in these shoes, this hat, out of doors, in all weathers, on every occasion. And to town.

I found a photograph of my son when he was twenty. He's in California with his friends, Erika and Elizabeth Lennard. He's thin, so thin you'd think he was a white Ugandan too. His smile strikes me as arrogant, derisive. He's trying to assume the warped image of a young drifter. That's how he likes to see himself, poor, with that poor boy's look, that attitude of someone young and thin. It's this photograph that comes closest to the one never taken of the girl on the ferry.

The one who bought the flat-brimmed pink hat with the broad black ribbon was her, the woman in another photograph, my mother. I recognize her better in that than in more recent photos. It's the courtyard of a house by the Small Lake in Hanoi. We're together, she and us, her children. I'm four years old. My mother's in the middle of the picture. I recognize the awkward way she holds herself, the way she doesn't smile, the way she waits for the photo to be over and done with. By her drawn face, by a certain untidiness in her dress, by her drowsy expression, I can tell that it's hot, that she's tired, that she's bored. But it's by the way we're dressed, us children, all anyhow, that I recognize a mood my mother sometimes used to fall into, and of which already, at the age we were in the photo, we knew the warning signs—the way she'd suddenly be unable to wash us, dress us, or sometimes even feed us. Every day my mother experienced this deep despondency about living. Sometimes it lasted, sometimes it would vanish with the dark. I had the luck to have a mother desperate with a despair so unalloyed that sometimes even life's happiness, at its most poignant, couldn't quite make her forget it. What I'll never know is what kind of practical considerations made her leave us like that, every day. This time, perhaps, it's the foolish thing she's just done, the house she's just bought—the one in the photograph—which we absolutely didn't need, and at a time when my father was already very ill, not far from death, only a few months. Or has she just learned she's got the same illness he is going to die of? The dates are right. What I don't know, and she can't have known either, is what kind of considerations they were that haunted her and made that dejection rise up before her. Was it the death, already at hand, of my father? Or the dying of the light? Doubts about her marriage? About her husband? About her children? Or about all these appurtenances in general?

It happened every day. Of that I'm sure. It must have come on quite suddenly. At a given moment every day the despair would make its appearance. And then would follow an inability to go on, or sleep, or sometimes nothing, or sometimes, instead, the buying of houses, the removals, or sometimes the moodiness, just the moodiness, the dejection. Or sometimes she'd be like a queen, give anything she was asked for, take anything she was offered, that house by the Small Lake, for absolutely no reason, my father already dying, or the flat-brimmed hat, because the girl had set her heart on it, or the same thing with the gold lamé shoes. Or else nothing, or just sleep, die.

I've never seen any of those films where American Indian women wear the same kind of flat-brimmed hat, with their hair in braids hanging down in front. That day I have braids too, not put up as usual, but not the same as theirs either. I too have a couple of long braids hanging down in front like those women in the films I've never seen, but mine are the braids of a child. Ever since I've had the hat, I've stopped putting my hair up so that I can wear it. For some time I've scraped my hair back to try to make it flat, so that people can't see it. Every night I comb and braid it before I go to bed, as my mother taught me. My hair is heavy, soft, burdensome, a coppery mass that comes down to my waist. People often say it's my prettiest feature, and I take that to mean I'm not pretty. I had this remarkable hair cut off when I was twenty-three, in Paris, five years after I left my mother. I said, "Cut it off." And he did. All at once, a clean sweep, I felt the cold scissors on the skin of my neck. It fell on the floor. They asked me if I wanted to keep it, they'd wrap it up for me to take away. I said no. After that people didn't say I had pretty hair any more, I mean not as much as they used to, before. Afterwards they'd just say, "She's got nice eyes. And her smile's not unattractive."

On the ferry, look, I've still got my hair. Fifteen and a half. I'm using make-up already. I use Crème Tokalon, and try to camouflage the freckles on my cheeks, under the eyes. On top of the Crème Tokalon I put natural-color powder—Houbigant. The powder is my mother's, she wears it to go to government receptions. That day I've got lipstick on too, dark red, cherry, as the fashion was then. I don't know where I got that, perhaps Hélène Lagonelle stole it for me from her mother, I forget. I'm not wearing perfume. My mother makes do with Palmolive and eau de Cologne.

On the ferry, beside the bus, there's a big black limousine with a chauffeur in white cotton livery. Yes, it's the big funereal car that's in my books. It's a Morris Léon-Bollée. The black Lancia at the French embassy in Calcutta hasn't yet made its entrance on the literary scene.

Between drivers and employers there are still sliding glass panels. There are still fold-down seats. A car is still as big as a bedroom.

Inside the limousine there's a very elegant man looking at me. He's not a white man. He's wearing European clothes—the light tussore suit of the Saigon bankers. He's looking at me. I'm used to people looking at me. People do look at white women in the colonies; at twelve-year-old white girls too. For the past three years white men, too, have been looking at me in the streets, and my mother's men friends have been kindly asking me to have tea with them while their wives are out playing tennis at the Sporting Club.

I could get it wrong, could think I'm beautiful like women who really are beautiful, like women who are looked at, just because people really do look at me a lot. I know it's not a question of beauty, though, but of something else, for example, yes, something else— mind, for example. What I want to seem I do seem, beautiful too if that's what people want me to be. Beautiful or pretty, pretty for the family for example, for the family no more than that. I can become any-thing anyone wants me to be. And believe it. Believe I'm charming too. And when I believe it, and it be-comes true for anyone seeing me who wants me to be according to his taste, I know that too. And so I can be deliberately charming even though I'm haunted by the killing of my brother. In that death, just one accom-plice, my mother. I use the word charming as people used to use it in relation to me, in relation to children.

I already know a thing or two. I know it's not clothes that make women beautiful or otherwise, nor beauty care, nor expensive creams, nor the distinction or costli-ness of their finery. I know the problem lies elsewhere. I don't know where. I only know it isn't where women think. I look at the women in the streets of Saigon, and upcountry. Some of them are very beautiful, very white, they take enormous care of their beauty here, especially upcountry. They don't do anything, just save themselves up, save themselves up for Europe, for lovers, holidays in Italy, the long six-months leaves every three years, when at last they'll be able to talk about what it's like here, this peculiar colonial existence, the marvelous domestic service provided by the houseboys, the vegetation, the dances, the white villas, big enough to get lost in, occupied by officials in distant outposts. They wait, these women. They dress just for the sake of dressing. They look at themselves. In the shade of their villas, they look at themselves for later on, they dream of romance, they already have huge wardrobes full of more dresses than they know what to do with, added to one by one like time, like the long days of waiting. Some of them go mad. Some are deserted for a young maid who keeps her mouth shut. Ditched. You can hear the word hit them, hear the sound of the blow. Some kill themselves.

This self-betrayal of women always struck me as a mistake, an error.

You didn't have to attract desire. Either it was in the woman who aroused it or it didn't exist. Either it was there at first glance or else it had never been. It was instant knowledge of sexual relationship or it was nothing. That too I knew before I experienced it.

Hélène Lagonelle was the only one who escaped the law of error. She was backward, a child still.

. . .

For a long time I've had no dresses of my own. My dresses are all a sort of sack, made out of old dresses of my mother's which themselves are all a sort of sack. Except for those my mother has made for me by Dô. She's the housekeeper who will never leave my mother even when she goes back to France, even when my elder brother tries to rape her in the house that goes with my mother's job in Sadec, even when her wages stop being paid. Dô was brought up by the nuns, she can embroider and do pleats, she can sew by hand as people haven't sewed by hand for centuries, with hair-fine needles. As she can embroider, my mother has her embroider sheets. As she can do pleats, my mother has her make me dresses with pleats, dresses with flounces, I wear them as if they were sacks, they're frumpish, childish, two sets of pleats in front and a Peter Pan collar, with a gored skirt or panels cut on the bias to make them look "professional." I wear these dresses as if they were sacks, with belts that take away their shape and make them timeless.

Fifteen and a half. The body is thin, undersized almost, childish breasts still, red and pale-pink make-up. And then the clothes, the clothes that might make people laugh, but don't. I can see it's all there. All there, but nothing yet done. I can see it in the eyes, all there already in the eyes. I want to write. I've already told my mother: That's what I want to do—write. No answer the first time. Then she asks, Write what? I say, Books, novels. She says grimly, When you've got your math degree you can write if you like, it won't be anything to do with me then. She's against it, it's not worthy, it's not real work, it's nonsense. Later she said, A childish idea.

The girl in the felt hat is in the muddy light of the river, alone on the deck of the ferry, leaning on the rails. The hat makes the whole scene pink. It's the only color. In the misty sun of the river, the sun of the hot season, the banks have faded away, the river seems to reach to the horizon. It flows quietly, without a sound, like the blood in the body. No wind but that in the water. The engine of the ferry is the only sound, a rickety old engine with burned-out rods. From time to time, in faint bursts, the sound of voices. And the barking of dogs, coming from all directions, from beyond the mist, from all the villages. The girl has known the ferryman since she was a child. He smiles at her and asks after her mother the headmistress, Madame la Directrice. He says he often sees her cross over at night, says she often goes to the property in Cambodia. Her mother is well, says the girl. All around the ferry is the river, it's brimfull, its moving waters sweep through, never mixing with, the stagnant waters of the rice fields. The river has picked up all it's met with since Tonle Sap and the Cambodian forest. It carries everything along, straw huts, forests, burned-out fires, dead birds, dead dogs, drowned tigers and buffalos, drowned men, bait, islands of water hyacinths all stuck together. Everything flows toward the Pacific, no time for anything to sink, all is swept along by the deep and headlong storm of the inner current, suspended on the surface of the river's strength.

I answered that what I wanted more than anything else in the world was to write, nothing else but that, nothing. Jealous. She's jealous. No answer, just a quick glance immediately averted, a slight shrug, unforgettable. I'll be the first to leave. There are still a few years to wait before she loses me, loses this one of her children. For the sons there's nothing to fear. But this one, she knows, one day she'll go, she'll manage to escape. Head of the class in French. The headmaster of the high school tells her, your daughter's head of the class in French, madame. My mother says nothing, nothing, she's cross because it's not her sons who are head of the class in French. The beast, my mother, my love, asks, What about math? Answer: Not yet, but it will come. My mother asks, When? Answer: When she makes up her mind to it, madame.

． ． ．

My mother, my love, her incredible ungainliness, with
her cotton stockings darned by Dô, in the tropics she
still thinks you have to wear stockings to be a lady, a
headmistress, her dreadful shapeless dresses, mended
by Dô, she's still straight out of her Picardy farm full
of female cousins, thinks you ought to wear everything
till it's worn out, that you have to be deserving, her
shoes, her shoes are down-at-heel, she walks awk-
wardly, painfully, her hair's drawn back tight into a
bun like a Chinese woman's, we're ashamed of her,
I'm ashamed of her in the street outside the school,
when she drives up to the school in her old Citroën B12
everyone looks, but she, she doesn't notice anything,
ever, she ought to be locked up, beaten, killed. She
looks at me and says, Perhaps you'll escape. Day and
night, this obsession. It's not that you have to achieve
anything, it's that you have to get away from where
you are.

When my mother emerges, comes out of her despair,
she sees the man's hat and the gold lamé shoes. She
asks what's it all about. I say nothing. She looks at me,
is pleased, smiles. Not bad, she says, they quite suit you,
make a change. She doesn't ask if it's she who bought
them, she knows she did. She knows she's capable of
it, that sometimes, those times I've mentioned, you can

get anything you like out of her, she can't refuse us anything. I say, Don't worry, they weren't expensive. She asks where. I say it was in the rue Catinat, marked-down markdowns. She looks at me with some fellow feeling. She must think it's a good sign, this show of imagination, the way the girl has thought of dressing like this. She not only accepts this buffoonery, this unseemliness, she, sober as a widow, dressed in dark colors like an unfrocked nun, she not only accepts it, she likes it.

The link with poverty is there in the man's hat too, for money has got to be brought in, got to be brought in somehow. All around her are wildernesses, wastes. The sons are wildernesses, they'll never do anything. The salt land's a wilderness too, the money's lost for good, it's all over. The only thing left is this girl, she's growing up, perhaps one day she'll find out how to bring in some money. That's why, though she doesn't know it, that's why the mother lets the girl go out dressed like a child prostitute. And that's why the child already knows how to divert the interest people take in her to the interest she takes in money. That makes her mother smile.

Her mother won't stop her when she tries to make money. The child will say, I asked him for five hundred piastres so that we can go back to France. Her mother will say, Good, that's what we'll need to set ourselves up in Paris, we'll be able to manage, she'll say, with five hundred piastres. The child knows what she's doing is what the mother would have chosen for her to do, if she'd dared, if she'd had the strength, if the pain of her thoughts hadn't been there every day, wearing her out.

In the books I've written about my childhood I can't remember, suddenly, what I left out, what I said. I think I wrote about our love for our mother, but I don't know if I wrote about how we hated her too, or about our love for one another, and our terrible hatred too, in that common family history of ruin and death which was ours whatever happened, in love or in hate, and which I still can't understand however hard I try, which is still beyond my reach, hidden in the very depths of my flesh, blind as a newborn child. It's the area on whose brink silence begins. What happens there is silence, the slow travail of my whole life. I'm still there, watching those possessed children, as far away from the mystery now as I was then. I've never written, though I thought I wrote, never loved, though I thought I loved, never done anything but wait outside the closed door.

.   .   .

When I'm on the Mekong ferry, the day of the black limousine, my mother hasn't yet given up the land by the dike. Every so often, still, we make the journey, at night, as before, still all three of us, to spend a few days there. We stay on the veranda of the bungalow, facing the mountains of Siam. Then we go home again. There's nothing she can do there, but she goes. My younger brother and I are beside her on the veranda overlooking the forest. We're too old now, we don't go bathing in the river any more, we don't go hunting black panther in the marshes in the estuary any more, or go into the forest, or into the villages in the pepper plantations. Everything has grown up all around us. There are no more children, either on the buffalos or anywhere else. We too have become strange, and the same sluggishness that has overtaken my mother has overtaken us too. We've learned nothing, watching the forest, waiting, weeping. The lower part of the land is lost for good and all, the servants work the patches higher up, we let them keep the paddy for themselves, they stay on without wages, making use of the stout straw huts my mother had built. They love us as if we were members of their own family, they act as if they were looking after the bungalow for us, and they do look after it. All the cheap crockery is still there. The roof, rotted by the endless rain, goes on disintegrating. But the furniture is kept polished. And the shape of the bungalow stands out clear as a diagram, visible from the road. The doors are opened every day to let the wind through and dry out the wood. And shut every night against stray dogs and smugglers from the mountains.

So you see it wasn't in the bar at Réam, as I wrote, that I met the rich man with the black limousine, it was after we left the land by the dike, two or three years after, on the ferry, the day I'm telling you about, in that light of haze and heat.

It's a year and a half after that meeting that my mother takes us back to France. She'll sell all her furniture. Then go one last time to the dike. She'll sit on the veranda facing the setting sun, look toward Siam one last time as she never will again, not even when she leaves France again, changes her mind again and comes back once more to Indochina and retires to Saigon. Never again will she go and see that mountain, that green and yellow sky above that forest.

Yes, I tell you, when she was already quite old she did it again. She opened a French-language school, the Nouvelle Ecole Française, which made enough for her to help me with my studies and to provide for her elder son as long as she lived.

. . .

My younger brother died in three days, of bronchial pneumonia. His heart gave out. It was then that I left my mother. It was during the Japanese occupation. Everything came to an end that day. I never asked her any more questions about our childhood, about herself. She died, for me, of my younger brother's death. So did my elder brother. I never got over the horror they inspired in me then. They don't mean anything to me any more. I don't know any more about them since that day. I don't even know how she managed to pay off her debts to the *chettis*, the Indian moneylenders. One day they stopped coming. I can see them now. They're sitting in the little parlor in Sadec wearing white dhotis, they sit there without saying a word, for months, years. My mother can be heard weeping and insulting them, she's in her room and won't come out, she calls out to them to leave her alone, they're deaf, calm, smiling, they stay where they are. And then one day, gone. They're dead now, my mother and my two brothers. For memories too it's too late. Now I don't love them any more. I don't remember if I ever did. I've left them. In my head I no longer have the scent of her skin, nor in my eyes the color of her eyes. I can't remember her voice, except sometimes when it grew soft with the weariness of evening. Her laughter I can't hear any more—neither her laughter nor her cries. It's over, I don't remember. That's why I can write about her so easily now, so long, so fully. She's become just something you write without difficulty, cursive writing.

She must have stayed on in Saigon from 1932 until 1949. It was in December 1942 that my younger brother died. She couldn't move any more. She stayed on—to be near the grave, she said. Then finally she came back to France. My son was two years old when we met again. It was too late for us to be reunited. We knew it at first glance. There was nothing left to reunite. Except for the elder son, all the rest was over. She went to live, and die, in the department of Loir-et-Cher, in the sham Louis XIV chateau. She lived there with Dô. She was still afraid at night. She bought a gun. Dô kept watch in the attics on the top floor. She also bought a place for her elder son near Amboise. With woods. He cut them down. Then went and gambled the money away in a baccarat club in Paris. The woods were lost in one night. The point at which my memory suddenly softens, and perhaps my brother brings tears to my eyes, is after the loss of the money from the woods. I know he's found lying in his car in Montparnasse, outside the Coupole, and that he wants to die. After that, I forget. What she did, my mother, with that chateau of hers, is simply unimaginable, still all for the sake of the elder son, the child of fifty incapable of earning any money. She buys some electric incubators and installs them in the main drawing room. Suddenly she's got six hundred chicks, forty square meters of them. But she made a mistake with the infrared rays, and none of the chicks can eat, all six hundred of them have beaks that don't meet or won't close, they all starve to death and she gives up. I came to the chateau while the chicks were hatching, there were great rejoicings. Afterwards the stench of the dead chicks and their food was so awful I couldn't eat in my mother's chateau without throwing up.

She died between Dô and him she called her child, in her big bedroom on the first floor, where during heavy frosts she used to put the sheep to sleep, five or six sheep all around her bed, for several winters, her last.

It's there, in that last house, the one on the Loire, when she finally gives up her ceaseless to-ing and fro-ing, that I see the madness clearly for the first time. I see my mother is clearly mad. I see that Dô and my brother have always had access to that madness. But that I, no, I've never seen it before. Never seen my mother in the state of being mad. Which she was. From birth. In the blood. She wasn't ill with it, for her it was like health, flanked by Dô and her elder son. No one else but they realized. She always had lots of friends, she kept the same friends for years and years and was always making new ones, often very young, among the officials from upcountry, or later on among the people in Touraine, where there were some who had retired from the French colonies. She always had people around her, all her life, because of what they called her lively intelligence, her cheerfulness, and her peerless, indefatigable poise.

I don't know who took the photo with the despair. The one in the courtyard of the house in Hanoi. Perhaps my father, one last time. A few months later he'd be sent back to France because of his health. Before that he'd go to a new job, in Phnom Penh. He was only there a few weeks. He died in less than a year. My mother wouldn't go back with him to France, she stayed where she was, stuck there. In Phnom Penh. In the fine house overlooking the Mekong, once the palace of the king of Cambodia, in the midst of those terrifying grounds, acres of them, where my mother is afraid. At night she makes us afraid too. All four of us sleep in the same bed. She says she's afraid of the dark. It's in this house she'll hear of my father's death. She'll know about it before the telegram comes, the night before, because of a sign only she saw and could understand, because of the bird that called in the middle of the night, frightened and lost in the office in the north front of the palace, my father's office. It's there, too, a few days after her husband's death, that my mother finds herself face to face with her own father. She switches the light on. There he is, standing by the table in the big octagonal drawing room. Looking at her. I remember a shriek, a call. She woke us up, told us what had happened, how he was dressed, in his Sunday best, grey, how he stood, how he looked at her, straight at her. She said, I wasn't afraid. She ran toward the vanished image. Both of them died on the day and at the time of the bird or the image. Hence, no doubt, our admiration for our mother's knowledge, about everything, including all that had to do with death.

The elegant man has got out of the limousine and is smoking an English cigarette. He looks at the girl in the man's fedora and the gold shoes. He slowly comes over to her. He's obviously nervous. He doesn't smile to begin with. To begin with he offers her a cigarette. His hand is trembling. There's the difference of race, he's not white, he has to get the better of it, that's why he's trembling. She says she doesn't smoke, no thanks. She doesn't say anything else, doesn't say, Leave me alone. So he's less afraid. He tells her he must be dreaming. She doesn't answer. There's no point in answering, what would she say? She waits. So he asks,

But where did you spring from? She says she's the daughter of the headmistress of the girls' school in Sadec. He thinks for a moment, then says he's heard of the lady, her mother, of her bad luck with the land they say she bought in Cambodia, is that right? Yes, that's right.

He says again how strange it is to see her on this ferry. So early in the morning, a pretty girl like that, you don't realize, it's very surprising, a white girl on a native bus.

He says the hat suits her, suits her extremely well, that it's very . . . original . . . a man's hat, and why not? She's so pretty she can do anything she likes.

She looks at him. Asks him who he is. He says he's just back from Paris where he was a student, that he lives in Sadec too, on this same river, the big house with the big terraces with blue-tiled balustrades. She asks him what he is. He says he's Chinese, that his family's from North China, from Fushun. Will you allow me to drive you where you want to go in Saigon? She says she will. He tells the chauffeur to get the girl's luggage off the bus and put it in the black car.

Chinese. He belongs to the small group of financiers of Chinese origin who own all the working-class housing in the colony. He's the one who was crossing the Mekong that day in the direction of Saigon.

. . .

She gets into the black car. The door shuts. A barely discernible distress suddenly seizes her, a weariness, the light over the river dims, but only slightly. Everywhere, too, there's a very slight deafness, or fog.

Never again shall I travel in a native bus. From now on I'll have a limousine to take me to the high school and back from there to the boarding school. I shall dine in the most elegant places in town. And I'll always have regrets for everything I do, everything I've gained, everything I've lost, good and bad, the bus, the bus driver I used to laugh with, the old women chewing betel in the back seats, the children on the luggage racks, the family in Sadec, the awfulness of the family in Sadec, its inspired silence.

He talked. Said he missed Paris, the marvelous girls there, the riotous living, the binges, ooh là là, the Coupole, the Rotonde, personally I prefer the Rotonde, the nightclubs, the "wonderful" life he'd led for two years. She listened, watching out for anything to do with his wealth, for indications as to how many millions he had. He went on. His own mother was dead, he was an only child. All he had left was his father, the one who owned the money. But you know how it is, for the last ten years he's been sitting staring at the river, glued to his opium pipe, he manages his money from his little iron cot. She says she sees.

He won't let his son marry the little white whore from Sadec.

The image starts long before he's come up to the white child by the rails, it starts when he got out of the black car, when he began to approach her, and when she knew, knew he was afraid.

From the first moment she knows more or less, knows he's at her mercy. And therefore that others besides him may be at her mercy too if the occasion arises. She knows something else too, that the time has now probably come when she can no longer escape certain duties toward herself. And that her mother will know nothing of this, nor her brothers. She knows this now too. As soon as she got into the black car she knew: she's excluded from the family for the first time and forever. From now on they will no longer know what becomes of her. Whether she's taken away from them, carried off, wounded, spoiled, they will no longer know. Neither her mother nor her brothers. That is their fate henceforth. It's already enough to make you weep, here in the black limousine.

Now the child will have to reckon only with this man, the first, the one who introduced himself on the ferry.

．．．

It happened very quickly that day, a Thursday. He'd come every day to pick her up at the high school and drive her back to the boarding school. Then one Thursday afternoon, the weekly half-holiday, he came to the boarding school and drove off with her in the black car.

It's in Cholon. Opposite the boulevards linking the Chinese part of the city to the center of Saigon, the great American-style streets full of streetcars, rickshaws, and buses. It's early in the afternoon. She's got out of the compulsory outing with the other girls.

It's a native housing estate to the south of the city. His place is modern, hastily furnished from the look of it, with furniture supposed to be ultra-modern. He says, I didn't choose the furniture. It's dark in the studio, but she doesn't ask him to open the shutters. She doesn't feel anything in particular, no hate, no repugnance either, so probably it's already desire. But she doesn't know it. She agreed to come as soon as he asked her the previous evening. She's where she has to be, placed here. She feels a tinge of fear. It's as if this must be not only what she expects, but also what had to happen especially to her. She pays close attention to externals, to the light, to the noise of the city in which the room is immersed. He's trembling. At first he looks at her as though he expects her to speak, but she doesn't. So he doesn't do anything either, doesn't undress her, says he loves her madly, says it very softly. Then is silent. She doesn't answer. She could say she doesn't love him. She says nothing. Suddenly, all at once, she knows, knows that he doesn't understand her, that he never will, that he lacks the power to understand such perverseness. And that he can never move fast enough to catch her. It's up to her to know. And she does. Because of his ignorance she suddenly knows: she was attracted to him already on the ferry. She was attracted to him. It depended on her alone.

She says, I'd rather you didn't love me. But if you do, I'd like you to do as you usually do with women. He looks at her in horror, asks, Is that what you want? She says it is. He's started to suffer here in this room, for the first time, he's no longer lying about it. He says he knows already she'll never love him. She lets him say it. At first she says she doesn't know. Then she lets him say it.

He says he's lonely, horribly lonely because of this love he feels for her. She says she's lonely too. She doesn't say why. He says, You've come here with me as you might have gone anywhere with anyone. She says she can't say, so far she's never gone into a bedroom with anyone. She tells him she doesn't want him to talk, what she wants is for him to do as he usually does with the women he brings to his flat. She begs him to do that.

He's torn off the dress, he throws it down. He's torn off her little white cotton panties and carries her over like that, naked, to the bed. And there he turns away and weeps. And she, slow, patient, draws him to her and starts to undress him. With her eyes shut. Slowly. He makes as if to help her. She tells him to keep still. Let me do it. She says she wants to do it. And she does. Undresses him. When she tells him to, he moves his body in the bed, but carefully, gently, as if not to wake her.

The skin is sumptuously soft. The body. The body is thin, lacking in strength, in muscle, he may have been ill, may be convalescent, he's hairless, nothing masculine about him but his sex, he's weak, probably a helpless prey to insult, vulnerable. She doesn't look him in the face. Doesn't look at him at all. She touches him. Touches the softness of his sex, his skin, caresses his goldenness, the strange novelty. He moans, weeps. In dreadful love.

And, weeping, he makes love. At first, pain. And then the pain is possessed in its turn, changed, slowly drawn away, borne toward pleasure, clasped to it.

The sea, formless, simply beyond compare.

．　．　．

Already, on the ferry, in advance, the image owed something to this moment.

The image of the woman in darned stockings has crossed the room, and at last she emerges as a child. The sons knew it already. But not the daughter, yet. They'd never talk about the mother among themselves, about the knowledge of her which they both shared and which separated them from her: the final, decisive knowledge that their mother was a child.

Their mother never knew pleasure.

I didn't know you bled. He asks me if it hurt, I say no, he says he's glad.

He wipes the blood away, washes me. I watch him. Little by little he comes back, becomes desirable again. I wonder how I had the strength to go against my mother's prohibition. So calmly, with such determination. How I managed to follow my ideas to their "logical conclusion."

We look at each other. He puts his arms around me. Asks me why I came here. I say I had to, it was a sort of obligation. It's the first time we've talked. I tell him I have two brothers. That we haven't any money. All gone. He knows my elder brother, has met him in the local opium dens. I say my brother steals from my mother to go there, steals from the servants, and that sometimes the keepers of the dens come and demand money from my mother. I tell him about the dikes. I tell him my mother will die, it can't go on like this. That my mother's approaching death, too, must be connected with what has happened to me today.

I notice that I desire him.

He feels sorry for me, but I say no, I'm not to be pitied, no one is, except my mother. He says, You only came because I'm rich. I say that's how I desire him, with his money, that when I first saw him he was already in his car, in his money, so I can't say what I'd have done if he'd been different. He says, I wish I could take you away, go away with you. I say I couldn't leave my mother yet without dying of grief. He says he certainly hasn't been lucky with me, but he'll give me some money anyway, don't worry. He's lain down again. Again we're silent.

The noise of the city is very loud, in recollection it's like the sound track of a film turned up too high, deafening. I remember clearly, the room is dark, we don't speak, it's surrounded by the continuous din of the city, caught up in the city, swept along with it. There are no panes in the windows, just shutters and blinds. On the blinds you can see the shadows of people going by in the sunlight on the sidewalks. Great crowds of them always. The shadows are divided into strips by the slats of the shutters. The clatter of wooden clogs is earsplitting, the voices strident, Chinese is a language that's shouted the way I always imagine desert languages are, it's a language that's incredibly foreign.

Outside it's the end of the day, you can tell by the sound of the voices, the sound of more and more passers-by, more and more miscellaneous. It's a city of pleasure that reaches its peak at night. And night is beginning now, with the setting sun.

The bed is separated from the city by those slatted shutters, that cotton blind. There's nothing solid separating us from other people. They don't know of our existence. We glimpse something of theirs, the sum of their voices, of their movements, like the intermittent hoot of a siren, mournful, dim.

Whiffs of burnt sugar drift into the room, the smell of roasted peanuts, Chinese soups, roast meat, herbs, jasmine, dust, incense, charcoal fires, they carry fire about in baskets here, it's sold in the street, the smell of the city is the smell of the villages upcountry, of the forest.

I suddenly saw him in a black bathrobe. He was sitting drinking a whisky, smoking.

He said I'd been asleep, he'd taken a shower. I'd fallen asleep almost unawares. He'd switched on a lamp on a low table.

He's a man of habit—I suddenly think of him—he

must come to this room quite often, he's a man who must make love a lot, a man who's afraid, he must make love a lot to fight against fear. I tell him I like the idea of his having many women, the idea of my being one of them, indistinguishable. We look at each other. He understands what I've just said. Our expressions are suddenly changed, false, caught in evil and death.

I tell him to come over to me, tell him he must possess me again. He comes over. He smells pleasantly of English cigarettes, expensive perfume, honey, his skin has taken on the scent of silk, the fruity smell of silk tussore, the smell of gold, he's desirable. I tell him of this desire. He tells me to wait awhile. Talks to me, says he knew right away, when we were crossing the river, that I'd be like this after my first lover, that I'd love love, he says he knows now I'll deceive him and deceive all the men I'm ever with. He says as for him he's been the cause of his own unhappiness. I'm pleased with all he's foretold, and say so. He becomes rough, desperate, he throws himself on me, devours the childish breasts, shouts, insults. I close my eyes on the intense pleasure. I think, He's used to it, this is his occupation in life, love, nothing else. His hands are expert, marvelous, perfect. I'm very lucky, obviously, it's as if it were his profession, as if unwittingly he knew exactly what to do and what to say. He calls me a whore, a slut, he says I'm his only love, and that's what he ought to say, and what you do say when you just let things say themselves, when you let the body alone, to seek and find and take what it likes, and then everything is right, and nothing's wasted, the waste is covered over and all is swept away in the torrent, in the force of desire.

The sound of the city is so near, so close, you can hear it brushing against the wood of the shutters. It sounds as if they're all going through the room. I caress his body amid the sound, the passers-by. The sea, the immensity, gathering, receding, returning.

I asked him to do it again and again. Do it to me. And he did, did it in the unctuousness of blood. And it really was unto death. It has been unto death.

He lit a cigarette and gave it to me. And very quietly, close to my lips, he talked to me.

And I talked to him too, very quietly.

Because he doesn't know for himself, I say it for him, in his stead. Because he doesn't know he carries within him a supreme elegance, I say it for him.

Now evening comes. He tells me I'll remember this afternoon all my life, even when I've forgotten his face and name. I wonder if I'll remember the house. He says, Take a good look at it. I do. I say it's like everywhere else. He says yes, yes, it's always the same.

I can still see the face, and I do remember the name. I see the whitewashed walls still, the canvas blind between us and the oven outside, the other door, arched, leading to the other room and to an open garden—the plants are dead from the heat—surrounded by blue balustrades like those at the big villa in Sadec with its tiers of terraces overlooking the Mekong.

It's a place of distress, shipwrecked. He asks me to tell him what I'm thinking about. I say I'm thinking about my mother, she'll kill me if she finds out the truth. I see he's making an effort, then he says it, says he understands what my mother means, this dishonor, he says. He says he himself couldn't bear the thought if it were a question of marriage. I look at him. He looks back, apologizes, proudly. He says, I'm Chinese. We smile at each other. I ask him if it's usual to be sad, as we are. He says it's because we've made love in the daytime, with the heat at its height. He says it's always terrible after. He smiles. Says, Whether people love one another or not, it's always terrible. Says it will pass as soon as it gets dark. I say he's wrong, it's not just because it was in the daytime, I feel a sadness I expected and which comes only from myself. I say I've always been sad. That I can see the same sadness in photos of myself when I was small. That today, recognizing it as the sadness I've always had, I could almost call it by my own name, it's so like me. Today I tell him it's a comfort, this sadness, a comfort to have fallen at last into a misfortune my mother has always predicted for me when she shrieks in the desert of her life. I say I don't quite understand what she says, but I know this room is what I was expecting. I speak without waiting for an answer. I tell him my mother shouts out what she believes like the messengers of God. She shouts that you shouldn't expect anything, ever, either from anybody else or from any government or from any God. He watches me speak, doesn't take his eyes off me, watches my lips, I'm naked, he caresses me, perhaps he's not listening, I don't know. I say I don't regard my present misfortune as a personal matter. I tell him how it was just so difficult to get food and clothes, to live, in short, on nothing but my mother's salary. I'm finding it more and more difficult to speak. He says, How did you all manage? I say we lived out of doors, poverty had knocked down the walls of the family and we were all left outside, each one fending for himself. Shameless, that's what we were. That's how I came to be here with you. He is on me, engulfed again. We stay like that, riveted, moaning amid the din of the still external city. We can still hear it. And then we don't hear it any more.

Kisses on the body bring tears. Almost like a consolation. At home I don't cry. But that day in that room, tears console both for the past and for the future. I tell him one day I'll leave my mother, one day even for my mother I'll have no love left. I weep. He lays his head on me and weeps to see me weep. I tell him that when I was a child my mother's unhappiness took the place of dreams. My dreams were of my mother, never of Christmas trees, always just her, a mother either flayed by poverty or distraught and muttering in the wilderness, either searching for food or endlessly telling what's happened to her, Marie Legrand from Roubaix, telling of her innocence, her savings, her hopes.

Through the shutters evening has come. The noise has got louder. It's more penetrating, less muffled. The livid red streetlights are lit.

We've left the flat. I've put on the man's hat with the black ribbon again, the gold shoes, the dark lipstick, the silk dress. I've grown older. I suddenly know it. He sees it, he says, You're tired.

On the sidewalk the crowd, going in all directions, slow or fast, forcing its way, mangy as stray dogs, blind as beggars, a Chinese crowd, I can still see it now in pictures of present prosperity, in the way they go along together without any sign of impatience, in the way they are alone in a crowd, without happiness, it seems, without sadness, without curiosity, going along without seeming to, without meaning to, just going this way rather than that, alone and in the crowd, never alone even by themselves, always alone even in the crowd.

We go to one of those Chinese restaurants on several floors, they occupy whole buildings, they're as big as department stores, or barracks, they look out over the city from balconies and terraces. The noise that comes from these buildings is inconceivable in Europe, the noise of orders yelled out by the waiters, then taken up and yelled out by the kitchens. No one ever merely speaks. On the terraces there are Chinese orchestras. We go up to the quietest floor, the Europeans' floor, the menus are the same but there's less yelling. There are fans, and heavy draperies to deaden the noise.

I ask him to tell me about his father's money, how he got rich. He says it bores him to talk about money, but if I insist he'll tell me what he knows about his father's wealth. It all began in Cholon, with the housing estates for natives. He built three hundred of these "compartments," cheap semidetached dwellings let out for rent. Owns several streets. Speaks French with an affected Paris accent, talks money with perfect ease. He used to own some apartment blocks, but sold them to buy building land south of Cholon. Some rice fields in

Sadec were sold too, the son thinks. I ask about epidemics. Say I've seen whole streets of native compartments closed off overnight, the doors and windows nailed up, because of an epidemic of plague. He says there's not so much of it here, the rats are exterminated much more often than upcountry. All of a sudden he starts telling me some rigmarole about the compartments. They cost much less than either apartment blocks or detached houses, and meet the needs of working-class areas much better than separate dwellings. The people here like living close together, especially the poor, who come from the country and like living out of doors too, on the street. And you must try not to destroy the habits of the poor. His father has just built a whole series of compartments with covered balconies overlooking the street. This makes the streets very light and agreeable. People spend the whole day on these outside balconies. Sleep there, too, when it's very hot. I say I'd have liked to live on an outside balcony myself, when I was small it was my dream, to sleep out of doors.

Suddenly I have a pain. Very slight, almost imperceptible. It's my heartbeat, shifted into the fresh, keen wound he's made in me, he, the one who's talking to me, the one who also made the afternoon's pleasure. I don't hear what he's saying, I've stopped listening. He sees, stops. I tell him to go on. He does. I listen again. He says he thinks about Paris a lot. He thinks I'm very different from the girls in Paris, not nearly so nice. I say the compartments can't be as profitable as all that. He doesn't answer.

Throughout our affair, for a year and a half, we'd talk like this, never about ourselves. From the first we knew we couldn't possibly have any future in common, so we'd never speak of the future, we'd talk about day-to-day events, evenly, hitting the ball back and forth.

I tell him his visit to France was fatal. He agrees. Says he bought everything in Paris, his women, his acquaintances, his ideas. He's twelve years older than I, and this scares him. I listen to the way he speaks, makes mistakes, makes love even—with a sort of theatricality at once contrived and sincere.

I tell him I'm going to introduce him to my family. He wants to run away. I laugh.

He can only express his feelings through parody. I discover he hasn't the strength to love me in opposition to his father, to possess me, take me away. He often weeps because he can't find the strength to love beyond fear. His heroism is me, his cravenness is his father's money.

Whenever I mention my brothers he's overcome by this fear, as if unmasked. He thinks my people all expect a proposal of marriage. He knows he's lost, done for already in my family's eyes, that for them he can only become more lost, and as a result lose me.

He says he went to study at a business school in Paris,

he tells the truth at last, says he didn't do any work and his father stopped his allowance, sent him his return ticket, and he had to leave. This retreat is his tragedy. He didn't finish the course at the business school. He says he hopes to finish it here by correspondence.

The meetings with the family began with the big meals in Cholon. When my mother and brothers come to Saigon I tell him he has to invite them to the expensive Chinese restaurants they don't know, have never been to before.

These evenings are all the same. My brothers gorge themselves without saying a word to him. They don't look at him either. They can't. They're incapable of it. If they could, if they could make the effort to see him, they'd be capable of studying, of observing the elementary rules of society. During these meals my mother's the only one who speaks, she doesn't say much, especially the first few times, just a few comments about the dishes as they arrive, the exorbitant price, then silence. He, the first couple of times, plunges in and tries to tell the story of his adventures in Paris, but in vain. It's as if he hadn't spoken, as if nobody had heard. His attempt founders in silence. My brothers go on gorging. They gorge as I've never seen anyone else gorge, anywhere.

He pays. He counts out the money. Puts it in the saucer. Everyone watches. The first time, I remember, he lays out seventy-seven piastres. My mother nearly shrieks with laughter. We get up to leave. No one says thank you. No one ever says thank you for the excellent dinner, or hello, or goodbye, or how are you, no one ever says anything to anyone.

My brothers never will say a word to him, it's as if he were invisible to them, as if for them he weren't solid enough to be perceived, seen or heard. This is because he adores me, but it's taken for granted I don't love him, that I'm with him for the money, that I can't love him, it's impossible, that he could take any sort of treatment from me and still go on loving me. This because he's a Chinese, because he's not a white man. The way my elder brother treats my lover, not speaking to him, ignoring him, stems from such absolute conviction it acts as a model. We all treat my lover as he does. I myself never speak to him in their presence. When my family's there I'm never supposed to address a single word to him. Except, yes, except to give him a message. For example, after dinner, when my brothers tell me they want to go to the Fountain to dance and drink, I'm the one who has to tell him. At first he pretends he hasn't heard. And I, according to my elder brother's strategy, I'm not supposed to repeat what I've just said, not supposed to ask again, because that would be wrong, I'd be admitting he has a grievance. Quietly, as if between ourselves, he says he'd like to be alone with me for a while. He says it to end the agony. Then I'm still not supposed to catch what he says properly, one more treachery, as if by what he said he meant to object, to complain of my elder brother's behavior. So I'm still not supposed to answer him. But he goes on, says, is bold enough to say, Your mother's tired, look at her. And our mother does get drowsy after those fabulous Chinese dinners in Cholon. But I still don't answer. It's then I hear my brother's voice. He says something short, sharp, and final. My mother used to say, He's the one who speaks best out of all the three. After he's spoken, my brother waits. Everything comes to a halt. I recognize my lover's fear, it's the same as my younger brother's. He gives in. We go to the Fountain. My mother too. At the Fountain she goes to sleep.

In my elder brother's presence he ceases to be my lover. He doesn't cease to exist, but he's no longer anything to me. He becomes a burned-out shell. My desire obeys my elder brother, rejects my lover. Every time I see them together I think I can never bear the sight again. My lover's denied in just that weak body, just that weakness which transports me with pleasure. In my brother's presence he becomes an unmentionable outrage, a cause of shame who ought to be kept out of sight. I can't fight my brother's silent commands. I can when it concerns my younger brother. But when it concerns my lover I'm powerless against myself. Thinking about it now brings back the hypocrisy to my face, the absent-minded expression of someone who stares into space, who has other things to think about, but who just the same, as the slightly clenched jaws show, suffers and is exasperated at having to put up with this indignity just for the sake of eating well, in an expensive restaurant, which ought to be something quite normal. And surrounding the memory is the ghastly glow of the night of the hunter. It gives off a strident note of alarm, like the cry of a child.

No one speaks to him at the Fountain, either.

We all order Martells and Perrier. My brothers drink theirs straight off and order the same again. My mother and I give them ours. My brothers are soon drunk. But they still don't speak to him. Instead they start finding fault. Especially my younger brother. He complains that the place is depressing and there aren't any hostesses. There aren't many people at the Fountain on a weekday. I dance with him, with my younger brother. I don't dance with my elder brother, I've never danced with him. I was always held back by a sense of danger, of the sinister attraction he exerted on everyone, a disturbing sense of the nearness of our bodies.

We were strikingly alike, especially in the face.

The Chinese from Cholon speaks to me, he's on the brink of tears, he says, What have I done to them? I tell him not to worry, it's always like that, even among ourselves, no matter what the circumstances.

I'll explain when we are together again in the apartment. I tell him my elder brother's cold, insulting violence is there whatever happens to us, whatever comes our way. His first impulse is always to kill, to wipe out, to hold sway over life, to scorn, to hunt, to make suffer. I tell him not to be afraid. He's got nothing to be afraid of. Because the only person my elder brother's afraid of, who, strangely, makes him nervous, is me.

Never a hello, a good evening, a happy New Year. Never a thank you. Never any talk. Never any need to talk. Everything always silent, distant. It's a family of stone, petrified so deeply it's impenetrable. Every day we try to kill one another, to kill. Not only do we not talk to one another, we don't even look at one another. When you're being looked at you can't look. To look is to feel curious, to be interested, to lower yourself. No one you look at is worth it. Looking is always demeaning. The word conversation is banished. I think that's what best conveys the shame and the pride. Every sort of community, whether of the family or other, is hateful to us, degrading. We're united in a fundamental shame at having to live. It's here we are at the heart of our common fate, the fact that all three of us are our mother's children, the children of a candid creature murdered by society. We're on the side of the society which has reduced her to despair. Because of what's been done to our mother, so amiable, so trusting, we hate life, we hate ourselves.

My mother didn't foresee what was going to become of us as a result of witnessing her despair. I'm speaking particularly of the boys, her sons. But even if she had foreseen it, how could she have kept quiet about what had become her own essential fate? How could she have made them all lie—her face, her eyes, her voice? Her love? She could have died. Done away with herself. Broken up our intolerable community. Seen to it that the eldest was completely separated from the younger two. But she didn't. She was careless, muddle-headed, irresponsible. All that. She went on living. And all three of us loved her beyond love. Just because she couldn't, because she wasn't able to keep quiet, hide things, lie, we, different as we all three were from one another, all three loved her in the same way.

·   ·   ·

It went on for a long time. Seven years. When it began we were ten. And then we were twelve. Then thirteen. Then fourteen, fifteen, Then sixteen, seventeen.

It lasted all that age, seven years. And then finally hope was given up. Abandoned. Like the struggles against the sea. From the shade of the veranda we look at the mountains of Siam, dark in broad daylight, almost black. My mother is quiet at last, mute. We, her children, are heroic, desperate.

My younger brother died in December 1942, during the Japanese occupation. I'd left Saigon after graduating from high school in 1931. He wrote to me just once in ten years. I never knew why. The letter was conventional, made out in a fair copy in careful handwriting without any mistakes. He told me everyone was well, the school was a success. It was a long letter, two whole pages. I recognized his writing, the same as when he was a child. He also said he had an apartment, a car, he told me the make. That he'd taken up tennis again. That he was fine, everything was fine. That he sent his fondest love. He didn't mention the war, or our elder brother.

I often bracket my two brothers together as she used to do, our mother. I say, My brothers, and she too, outside the family, used to say, My sons. She always talked in an insulting way about her sons' strength. For the outside world she didn't distinguish between them, she didn't say the elder son was much stronger than the younger, she said he was as strong as her brothers, the farmers in the North of France. She was proud of her sons' strength in the same way as she'd been proud of her brothers'. Like her elder son, she looked down on the weak. Of my lover from Cholon she spoke in the same way as my elder brother. I won't write the words down. They were words that had to do with the carrion you find in the desert. I say, My brothers, because that's what I used to say too. It was only afterwards that I referred to them differently, after my younger brother grew up and was martyred.

Not only do we never have any celebrations in our family, not a Christmas tree, or so much as an embroidered handkerchief or a flower. We don't even take notice of any death, any funeral, any remembrance. There's just her. My elder brother will always be a murderer. My younger brother will die because of him. As for me, I left, tore myself away. Until she died my elder brother had her to himself.

At that time, the time of Cholon, of the image, of the lover, my mother has an access of madness. She knows nothing of what's happened in Cholon. But I can see she's watching me, she suspects something. She knows her daughter, her child, and hovering around that child, for some time, there's been an air of strangeness, a sort of reserve, quite recent, that catches the eye. The girl speaks even more slowly than usual, she's absent-minded, she who's usually so interested in everything, her expression has changed, she's become a spectator even of her mother, of her mother's unhappiness, it's as if she were witnessing its outcome. There's a sudden terror in my mother's life. Her daughter's in the direst danger, the danger of never getting married, never having a place in society, of being defenseless against it, lost, alone. My mother has attacks during which she falls on me, locks me up in my room, punches me, undresses me, comes up to me and smells my body, my underwear, says she can smell the Chinese's scent, goes even further, looks for suspect stains on my underwear, and shouts, for the whole town to hear, that her daughter's a prostitute, she's going to throw her out, she wishes she'd die, no one will have anything to do with her, she's disgraced, worse than a bitch. And she weeps, asking what she can do, except drive her out of the house so she can't stink the place up any more.

Outside the walls of the locked room, my brother.

He answers my mother, tells her she's right to beat the girl, his voice is lowered, confidential, coaxing, he says they must find out the truth, at all costs, must find out in order to save the girl, save the mother from being driven to desperation. The mother hits her as hard as she can. The younger brother shouts at the mother to leave her alone. He goes out into the garden, hides, he's afraid I'll be killed, he's afraid, he's always afraid of that stranger, our elder brother. My younger brother's fear calms my mother down. She weeps for the disaster of her life, of her disgraced child. I weep with her. I lie. I swear by my own life that nothing has happened to me, nothing, not even a kiss. How could I, I say, with a Chinese, how could I do that with a Chinese, so ugly, such a weakling? I know my elder brother's glued to the door, listening, he knows what my mother's doing, he knows the girl's naked, being beaten, and he'd like it to go on and on to the brink of harm. My mother is not unaware of my elder brother's obscure and terrifying intent.

We're still very small. Battles break out regularly between my brothers, for no apparent reason except the classic one by which the elder brother says to the younger, Clear out, you're in the way. And straightway lashes out. They fight without a word, all you can hear is their breathing, their groans, the hollow thud of the blows. My mother accompanies this scene, like all others, with an opera of shrieks.

They both have the same talent for anger, those black, murderous fits of anger you only see in brothers,

sisters, mothers. My elder brother can't bear not being
able to do evil freely, to be boss over it not only here
but everywhere. My younger brother can't bear having
to look on helpless at this horror, at what his elder
brother is like.

When they fought we were equally afraid for both
of their lives. My mother used to say they'd always
fought, they'd never played together, never talked to
one another. That they had nothing in common but
her, their mother, and especially their sister. Nothing
but blood.

I believe it was only her eldest that my mother
called "my child." She sometimes called him that. The
other two she called "the younger ones."

We said nothing about all this outside, one of the
first things we'd learned was to keep quiet about the
ruling principle of our life, poverty. And then about
everything else. Our first confidants, though the word
seems excessive, are our lovers, the people we meet
away from our various homes, first in the streets of
Saigon and then on ocean liners and trains, and then all
over the place.

It takes my mother all of a sudden toward the end of
the afternoon, especially in the dry season, and then
she'll have the house scrubbed from top to bottom, to
clean it through, scour it out, freshen it up, she says.

The house is built on a raised strip of land, clear of the garden, the snakes, the scorpions, the red ants, the floodwaters of the Mekong, those that follow the great tornados of the monsoon. Because the house is raised like this it can be cleaned by having buckets of water thrown over it, sluiced right through like a garden. All the chairs are piled up on the tables, the whole house is streaming, water is lapping around the piano in the small sitting room. The water pours down the steps, spreads through the yard toward the kitchen quarters. The little houseboys are delighted, we join in with them, splash one another, then wash the floor with yellow soap. Everyone's barefoot, including our mother. She laughs. She's got no objection to anything. The whole house smells nice, with the delicious smell of wet earth after a storm, enough to make you wild with delight, especially when it's mixed with the other, the smell of yellow soap, of purity, of respectability, of clean linen, of whiteness, of our mother, of the immense candor and innocence of our mother. The houseboys' families come along, and the houseboys' visitors, and the white children from neighboring houses. My mother's very happy with this disorder, she can be very very happy sometimes, long enough to forget, the time it takes to clean out the house may be enough to make her happy. She goes into the sitting room, sits down at the piano, plays the only tunes she knows by heart, the ones she learned at the normal school. She sings. Sometimes she laughs while she plays. Gets up, dances, and sings. And everyone thinks, and so does she, that you can be happy here in this house suddenly transmogrified into a pond, a water meadow, a ford, a beach.

The two smaller children, the girl and the younger brother, are the first to remember. They suddenly stop laughing and go into the darkening garden.

I remember, just as I'm writing this, that our elder brother wasn't in Vinh Long when we sluiced the house out. He was living with our guardian, a village priest, in the department of Lot-et-Garonne. He too used to laugh sometimes, but never as much as we did. I forget everything, and I forgot to say this, that we were children who laughed, my younger brother and I, laughed fit to burst, fit to die.

I see the war as I see my childhood. I see wartime and the reign of my elder brother as one. Partly, no doubt, because it was during the war that my younger brother died: his heart, as I've said, had given out, given up. As for my elder brother, I don't think I ever saw him during the war. By that time it didn't matter to me whether he was alive or dead. I see the war as like him, spreading everywhere, breaking in everywhere, stealing, imprisoning, always there, merged and mingled with everything, present in the body, in the mind, awake and asleep, all the time, a prey to the intoxicating passion of occupying that delightful territory, a child's body, the bodies of those less strong, of conquered peoples. Because evil is there, at the gates, against the skin.

We go back to the apartment. We are lovers. We can't stop loving each other.

Sometimes I don't go back to the boarding school. I sleep with him. I don't want to sleep in his arms, his warmth, but I do sleep in the same room, the same bed. Sometimes I stay away from high school. At night we go and have dinner in town. He gives me my shower, washes me, rinses me, he adores that, he puts my make-up on and dresses me, he adores me. I'm the darling of his life. He lives in terror lest I meet another man. I'm never afraid of anything like that. He's also afraid, not because I'm white, but because I'm so young, so young he could go to prison if we were found out. He tells me to go on lying to my mother, and above all to my elder brother, never to say anything to anyone. I go on lying. I laugh at his fear. I tell him we're much too poor for my mother to start another lawsuit, and anyway she's lost all those she ever did start, against the land registrar, against the officials, the government, the law, she doesn't know how to conduct them properly, how to keep calm, wait, go on waiting, she can't, she makes a scene and spoils her chances. With this one it would be the same, so no need to be afraid.

Marie-Claude Carpenter. She was American—from Boston, I seem to remember. Very pale eyes, grey-blue. 1943. Marie-Claude Carpenter was fair. Scarcely faded. Quite good-looking, I think. With a brief smile that froze very quickly, disappeared in a flash. With a voice that suddenly comes back to me, low, slightly grating in the high notes. She was forty-five, old already, old age itself. She lived in the sixteenth arrondissement, near the place de l'Alma. Her apartment was the huge top floor of a block overlooking the Seine. People went to dinner there in the winter. Or to lunch in the summer. The meals were ordered from the best caterers in Paris. Always passable, almost. But only just enough, skimpy. She was never seen anywhere else but at home, never out. Sometimes there was an expert on Mallarmé there. And often one, two, or three literary people, they'd come once and never be seen again. I never found out where she got them from, where she met them, or why she invited them. I never heard anyone else refer to any of them, and I never read or heard of their work. The meals didn't last very long. We talked a lot about the war, it was the time of Stalingrad, the end of the winter of '42. Marie-Claude

Carpenter used to listen a lot, ask a lot of questions, but
didn't say much, often used to express surprise at how
little she knew of what went on, then she'd laugh.
Straightway after the meal she'd apologize for having
to leave so soon, but she had things to do, she said. She
never said what. When there were enough of us we'd
stay on for an hour or two after she left. She used to say,
Stay as long as you like. No one spoke about her when
she wasn't there. I don't think anyone could have,
because no one knew her. You always went home with
the feeling of having experienced a sort of empty night-
mare, of having spent a few hours as the guest of
strangers with other guests who were strangers too, of
having lived through a space of time without any
consequences and without any cause, human or other.
It was like having crossed a third frontier, having been
on a train, having waited in doctors' waiting rooms,
hotels, airports. In summer we had lunch on a big
terrace looking over the river, and coffee was served
in the garden covering the whole roof. There was a
swimming pool. But no one went in. We just sat and
looked at Paris. The empty avenues, the river, the
streets. In the empty streets, catalpas in flower. Marie-
Claude Carpenter. I looked at her a lot, practically all
the time, it embarrassed her but I couldn't help it. I
looked at her to try to find out, find out who she was,
Marie-Claude Carpenter. Why she was there rather
than somewhere else, why she was from so far away

too, from Boston, why she was rich, why no one knew anything about her, not anything, no one, why these seemingly compulsory parties. And why, why, in her eyes, deep down in the depths of sight, that particle of death? Marie-Claude Carpenter. Why did all her dresses have something indefinable in common that made them look as if they didn't quite belong to her, as if they might just as well have been on some other body? Dresses that were neutral, plain, very light in color, white, like summer in the middle of winter.

Betty Fernandez. My memory of men is never lit up and illuminated like my memory of women. Betty Fernandez. She was a foreigner too. As soon as I say the name there she is, walking along a Paris street, she's short-sighted, can't see much, screws up her eyes to recognize you, then greets you with a light hand-shake. Hello, how are you? Dead a long time ago now. Thirty years, perhaps. I can remember her grace, it's too late now for me to forget, nothing mars its perfection still, nothing ever will, not the circumstances, nor the time, nor the cold or the hunger or the defeat of Germany, nor the coming to light of the crime. She goes along the street still, above the history of such things however terrible. Here too the eyes are pale. The pink dress is old, the black wide-brimmed hat dusty in the sunlight of the street.

She's slim, tall, drawn in India ink, an engraving. People stop and look in amazement at the elegance of this foreigner who walks along unseeing. Like a queen. People never know at first where she's from. And then they think she can only be from somewhere else, from there. Because of this she's beautiful. She's dressed in old European clothes, scraps of brocade, out-of-date old suits, old curtains, old oddments, old models, moth-eaten old fox furs, old otterskins, that's her kind of beauty, tattered, chilly, plaintive and in exile, nothing suits her, everything's too big, and yet it looks marvelous. Her clothes are loose, she's too thin, nothing fits, yet it looks marvelous. She's made in such a way, face and body, that anything that touches her shares immediately and infallibly in her beauty.

She entertained, Betty Fernandez, she had an "at home." We went sometimes. Once Drieu La Rochelle was there. Clearly suffering from pride, he scarcely deigned to speak, and when he did it was as if his voice was dubbed, his words translated, stiff. Maybe Brasillach was there too, but I don't remember, unfortunately. Sartre never came. There were poets from Montparnasse, but I don't remember any names, not one. There were no Germans. We didn't talk politics. We talked about literature. Ramon Fernandez used to talk about Balzac. We could have listened to him forever and a day. He spoke with a knowledge that's almost completely forgotten, and of which almost nothing completely verifiable can survive. He offered opinions rather than information. He spoke about Balzac as he might have done about himself, as if he himself had once tried to be Balzac. He had a sublime courtesy even in knowledge, a way at once profound and clear of handling knowledge without ever making it seem an obligation or a burden. He was sincere. It was always a joy to meet him in the street or in a café, and it was a pleasure to him to greet you. Hallo how are you? he'd say, in the English style, without a comma, laughing. And while he laughed his jest became the war itself, together with all the unavoidable suffering it caused, both resistance and collaboration, hunger and cold, martyrdom and infamy. She, Betty Fernandez, spoke only of people, those she'd seen in the street or those she knew, about how they were, the things still left for sale in the shops, extra rations of milk or fish, good ways of dealing with shortages, with cold and constant hunger, she was always concerned with the practical details of life, she didn't go beyond that, always a good friend, very loyal and affectionate. Collaborators, the Fernandezes were. And I, two years after the war, I was a member of the French Communist party. The parallel is complete and absolute. The two things are the same, the same pity, the same call for help, the same lack of judgment, the same superstition if you like, that consists in believing in a political solution to the personal problem. She too, Betty Fernandez, looked out at the empty streets of the German occupation, looked at Paris, at the squares of catalpas in flower, like the other woman, Marie-Claude Carpenter. Was "at home" certain days, like her.

He drives her back to the boarding school in the black limousine. Stops just short of the entrance so that no one sees him. It's at night. She gets out, runs off, doesn't turn to look at him. As soon as she's inside the door she sees the lights are still on in the big playground. As soon as she turns out of the corridor she sees her, waiting for her, worried already, erect, unsmiling. She asks, Where've you been? She says, I just didn't come back here to sleep. She doesn't say why and Hélène Lagonelle doesn't ask. She takes the pink hat off and undoes her braids for the night. You didn't go to class either. No, she didn't. Hélène says they've phoned, that's how she knows, she's to go and see the vice-principal. There are lots of girls in the shadowy playground. They're all in white. There are big lamps in the trees. The lights are still on in some of the classrooms. Some of the pupils are working late, others stay in the classrooms to chat, or play cards, or sing. There's no fixed time for them to go to bed, it's so hot during the day they're allowed to do more or less as they like in the evening, or rather as the young teachers on duty like. We're the only two white girls in this state boarding school. There are lots of half-castes, most of them abandoned by their fathers, soldiers or sailors or minor officials in the customs, post, or public works department. Most of them were brought up by the Assistance Board. There are a few quadroons too. Hélène Lagonelle believes the French government raises them to be nurses in hospitals or to work in orphanages, leper colonies, and mental homes. She also thinks they're sent to isolation hospitals to look after people with cholera or the plague. That's what Hélène Lagonelle thinks, and she cries because she doesn't want any of those jobs, she's always talking about running away.

I go to see the teacher on duty, a young half-caste herself who spends a lot of time looking at Hélène and me. She says, You didn't go to class and you didn't sleep here last night, we're going to have to inform your mother. I say I couldn't help it, but from now on I'll try to come back and sleep here every night, there's no need to tell my mother. The young woman looks at me and smiles.

I'll do it again. My mother will be informed. She'll come and see the head of the boarding school and ask her to let me do as I like in the evenings, not to check the time I come in, not to force me to go out with the other girls on Sunday excursions. She says, She's a child who's always been free, otherwise she'd run away, even I, her own mother, can't do anything about it, if I want to keep her I have to let her be free. The head agrees because I'm white and the place needs a few whites among all the half-castes for the sake of its reputation. My mother also said I was working hard in high school even though I had my freedom, and that what had happened with her sons was so awful, such a disaster, that her daughter's education was the only hope left to her.

The head let me live in the boarding school as if it were a hotel.

Soon I'll have a diamond on my engagement finger. Then the teachers will stop making remarks. People will guess I'm not engaged, but the diamond's very valuable, no one will doubt that it's genuine, and no one will say anything any more, because of the value of the diamond that's been given to this very young girl.

I come back to Hélène Lagonelle. She's lying on a bench, crying because she thinks I'm going to leave. I sit on the bench. I'm worn out by the beauty of Hélène Lagonelle's body lying against mine. Her body is sublime, naked under the dress, within arm's reach. Her breasts are such as I've never seen. I've never touched them. She's immodest, Hélène Lagonelle, she doesn't realize, she walks around the dormitories without any clothes on. The most beautiful of all the things given by God is this body of Hélène Lagonelle's, peerless, the balance between her figure and the way the body bears the breasts, outside itself, as if they were separate. Nothing could be more extraordinary than the outer roundness of these breasts proffered to the hands, this outwardness held out toward them. Even the body of my younger brother, like that of a little coolie, is as nothing beside this splendor. The shapes of men's bodies are miserly, internalized. Nor do they get spoiled like those of such girls as Hélène Lagonelle, which never last, a summer or so perhaps, that's all. She comes from the high plateaus of Da Lat. Her father works for the post office. She came quite recently, right in the middle of the school year. She's frightened, she comes up and sits beside you and stays there without speaking, crying sometimes. She has the pink-and-brown complexion of the mountains, you can always recognize it here where all the other children are pale green with anemia and the torrid heat. Hélène Lagonelle doesn't go to high school. She's not capable of it, Hélène L. She can't learn, can't remember things. She goes to the primary classes at the boarding school, but it's no use. She weeps up against me, and I stroke her hair, her hands, tell her I'm going to stay here with her. She doesn't know she's very beautiful, Hélène

Lagonelle. Her parents don't know what to do with her, they want to marry her off as soon as possible. She could have all the fiancés she likes, Hélène Lagonelle, but she doesn't like, she doesn't want to get married, she wants to go back to her mother. She, Hélène L. Hélène Lagonelle. In the end she'll do what her mother wants. She's much more beautiful than I am, the girl in the clown's hat and lamé shoes, infinitely more marriageable, she can be married off, set up in matrimony, you can frighten her, explain it to her, what frightens her and what she doesn't understand, tell her to stay where she is, wait.

Hélène Lagonelle is seventeen, seventeen, yet she still doesn't know what I know. It's as if I guessed she never will.

Hélène Lagonelle's body is heavy, innocent still, her skin's as soft as that of certain fruits, you almost can't grasp her, she's almost illusory, it's too much. She makes you want to kill her, she conjures up a marvelous dream of putting her to death with your own hands. Those flour-white shapes, she bears them unknowingly, and offers them for hands to knead, for lips to eat, without holding them back, without any knowledge of them and without any knowledge of their fabulous power. I'd like to eat Hélène Lagonelle's breasts as he eats mine in the room in the Chinese town where I go every night to increase my knowledge of God. I'd like to devour and be devoured by those flour-white breasts of hers.

I am worn out with desire for Hélène Lagonelle.

I am worn out with desire.

I want to take Hélène Lagonelle with me to where every evening, my eyes shut, I have imparted to me the pleasure that makes you cry out. I'd like to give Hélène Lagonelle to the man who does that to me, so he may do it in turn to her. I want it to happen in my presence, I want her to do it as I wish, I want her to give herself where I give myself. It's via Hélène Lagonelle's body, through it, that the ultimate pleasure would pass from him to me.

A pleasure unto death.

I see her as being of one flesh with the man from Cholon, but in a shining, solar, innocent present, in a continual self-flowering which springs out of each action, each tear, each of her faults, each of her ignorances. Hélène Lagonelle is the mate of the bondsman who gives me such abstract, such harsh pleasure, the obscure man from Cholon, from China. Hélène Lagonelle is from China.

I haven't forgotten Hélène Lagonelle. I haven't forgotten the bondsman. When I went away, when I left him, I didn't go near another man for two years. But that mysterious fidelity must have been to myself.

I'm still part of the family, it's there I live, to the exclusion of everywhere else. It's in its aridity, its terrible harshness, its malignance, that I'm most deeply sure of myself, at the heart of my essential certainty, the certainty that later on I'll be a writer.

That's the place where later on, once the present is left behind, I must stay, to the exclusion of everywhere else. The hours I spend in the apartment show it in a new light. It's a place that's intolerable, bordering on death, a place of violence, pain, despair, dishonor. And so is Cholon. On the other bank of the river. As soon as you've crossed to the other side.

I don't know what became of Hélène Lagonelle, I don't even know if she's dead. It was she who left the boarding school first, a long while before I went to France. She went back to Da Lat. Her mother sent for her, I believe to arrange a match for her, I believe she was to meet someone just out from France. But I may be wrong, I may be projecting what I thought would happen to Hélène Lagonelle onto her prompt departure at her mother's request.

Let me tell you what he did, too, what it was like. Well—he stole from the houseboys in order to go and smoke opium. He stole from our mother. He rummaged in closets. He stole. He gambled. My father bought a house in Entre-Deux-Mers before he died. It was the only thing we owned. He gambles. My mother sells the house to pay his debts. But it isn't enough, it's never enough. When he's young he tries to sell me to customers at the Coupole. It's for him my mother wants to go on living, so he can go on eating, so he can have a roof over his head, so he can still hear someone call him by his name. Then there's the place she bought for him near Amboise, ten years' savings. Mortgaged in one night. She pays the interest. And all the profit from the cutting down of the woods I told you about. In one night. He stole from my mother when she was dying. He was the sort of person who rummaged in closets, who had a gift for it, knew where to look, could find the right piles of sheets, the hiding places. He stole wedding rings, that sort of thing, lots of them, jewelry, food. He stole from Dô, the houseboys, my younger brother. From me. Plenty. He'd have sold her, his own mother. When she dies he sends for the lawyer right away, in the midst of all the emotion. He takes advantage of it. The lawyer says the will is not valid. It favors the elder son too much at my expense. The difference is enormous, laughable. I have to refuse or accept, in full knowledge of the facts. I say I'll accept: I'll sign. I've accepted. My brother lowers his eyes. Thanks. He weeps. In the midst of all the emotion of our mother's death. He's quite sincere. At the liberation of Paris, probably on the run for having been a collaborator in the South, he has nowhere to go. He comes to me. He's running away from some danger, I never quite knew what. Perhaps he informed on people, Jews perhaps, anything is possible. He's very mild and affectionate, as always after he's committed murders or when he needs your help. My husband has been deported. He sympathizes. He stays three days. I've forgotten, and when I go out I don't lock anything up. He rummages around. I've been keeping my rice and sugar rations for when my husband comes back. He rummages around and takes them. He also rummages around in a little closet in my bedroom. He finds what he's looking for and takes all my savings, fifty thousand francs. He doesn't leave a single note. He quits the apartment with the spoils. When I see him again I won't mention it, it's too shaming for him, I couldn't. After the fake will, the fake Louis XIV chateau is sold for a song. The sale was a put-up job, like the will.

After my mother's death he's left alone. He has no

friends, never has had, sometimes he's had women who "worked" for him in Montparnasse, sometimes women who didn't work for him, at least to begin with, sometimes men, but then they did the paying. He lived a very lonely life. And more so as he grew older. He was only a layabout, he operated on a very small scale. He inspired fear in his immediate circle, but no farther. When he lost us he lost his real empire. He wasn't a gangster, just a family layabout, a rummager in closets, a murderer without a gun. He didn't take any risks. Layabouts all live as he did, without any loyalty, without any grandeur, in fear. He was afraid. After my mother's death he leads a strange existence. In Tours. The only people he knows are waiters in cafés, for the racing tips, and the bibulous patrons of backroom poker games. He starts to look like them, drinks a lot, gets bloodshot eyes and slurred speech. In Tours he had nothing. Both houses had been sold off. Nothing. For a year he lived in a furniture warehouse leased by my mother. For a year he slept in an armchair. They let him go there. Stay for a year. Then they threw him out.

For a year he must have hoped to buy his mortgaged property back. He gambled away my mother's furniture out of storage, bit by bit. The bronze Buddhas, the brasses, then the beds, then the wardrobes, then the sheets. And then one day he has nothing left, that does happen to people like him, one day he has the suit on his back and nothing else, not a sheet, not a shelter. He's alone. For a year no one will open their door to him. He writes to a cousin in Paris. He can have a servant's room in the boulevard Malesherbes. And when he's over fifty he'll have his first job, his first wages ever, as messenger for a marine insurance company. That lasted, I think, fifteen years. He had to go into the hospital. He didn't die there. He died in his room.

My mother never talked about that one of her children. She never mentioned the rummager in closets to anyone. She treated the fact that she was his mother as if it were a crime. She kept it hidden. She must have thought it was unintelligible, impossible to convey to anyone who didn't know her son as she did, before God and only before Him. She repeated little platitudes about him, always the same ones. That if he'd wanted to he could have been the cleverest of the three. The most "artistic." The most astute. And he was the one who'd loved his mother most. The one, in short, who'd understood her best. I didn't know, she'd say, that you could expect that of a boy, such intuition, such deep affection.

We met again once, he spoke about our dead brother. He said of his death, What an awful thing, how dreadful, our little brother, our little Paulo.

There remains this image of our kinship: a meal

in Sadec. All three of us are eating at the dining-room table. They're seventeen, eighteen. My mother's not with us. He watches us eat, my younger brother and me, then he puts down his fork and looks at my younger brother. For a very long time he looks at him, then suddenly, very calmly, says something terrible. About food. He says he must be careful, he shouldn't eat so much. My younger brother doesn't answer. The other goes on. Reminds him the big pieces of meat are for him, and he mustn't forget it. Or else, he says. I ask, Why are they for you? He says, Because that's how it is. I say, I wish you'd die. I can't eat any more. Nor can my younger brother. He waits for my younger brother to dare to speak, just one word, his clenched fists are poised ready over the table to bash his face in. My younger brother says nothing. He's very pale. Between his lashes, the beginning of tears.

It was a dreary day, the day he died. In spring, I think it was, April. Someone telephones. They don't say anything else, nothing, just that he's been found dead, on the floor, in his room. But death came before the end of his story. When he was still alive it had already happened, it was too late now for him to die, it had been all over since the death of my younger brother. The conquering words: It is finished.

She asked for him to be buried with her. I don't

know where, in which cemetery. I just know it's in the Loire. Both in the same grave. Just the two of them. It's as it should be. An image of intolerable splendor.

Dusk fell at the same time all the year round. It was very brief, almost like a blow. In the rainy season, for weeks on end, you couldn't see the sky, it was full of an unvarying mist which even the light of the moon couldn't pierce. In the dry season, though, the sky was bare, completely free of cloud, naked. Even moonless nights were light. And the shadows were as clear-cut as ever on the ground, and on the water, roads, and walls.

I can't really remember the days. The light of the sun blurred and annihilated all color. But the nights, I remember them. The blue was more distant than the sky, beyond all depths, covering the bounds of the world. The sky, for me, was the stretch of pure brilliance crossing the blue, that cold coalescence beyond all color. Sometimes, it was in Vinh Long, when my mother was sad she'd order the gig and we'd drive out into the country to see the night as it was in the dry season. I had that good fortune—those nights, that mother. The light fell from the sky in cataracts of pure transparency, in torrents of silence and immobility. The air was blue, you could hold it in your hand. Blue. The sky was the continual throbbing of the brilliance of the light. The night lit up everything, all the country on either bank of the river as far as the eye could reach. Every night was different, each one had a name as long as it lasted. Their sound was that of the dogs, the country dogs baying at mystery. They answered one another from village to village, until the time and space of the night were utterly consumed.

On the paths of the yard the shadows of the cinnamon-apple trees are inky black. The whole garden is still as marble. The house too—monumental, funereal. And my younger brother, who was walking beside me, now looks intently at the gate open on the empty road.

One day he's not there outside the high school. The driver's alone in the black car. He says the father's ill and the young master's gone back to Sadec. He, the driver, has been told to stay in Saigon to take me to school and back again to the boarding house. The young master came back after a few days. Again he was there in the back of the black car, his face averted so as not to see people looking at him, still afraid. We kissed, without a word, kissed there outside the school, we'd forgotten. While we kissed, he wept. His father was going to live. His last hope was vanishing.

He'd asked him, implored him to let him keep me with him, close to him, he'd told him he must understand, must have known a passion like this himself at least once in his long life, it couldn't be otherwise, he'd begged him to let him have his turn at living, just once, this passion, this madness, this infatuation with the little white girl, he'd asked him to give him time to love her a while longer before sending her away to France, let him have her a little longer, another year perhaps, because it wasn't possible for him to give up this love yet, it was too new, too strong still, too much in its first violence, it was too terrible for him to part yet from her body, especially since, as he the father knew, it could never happen again.

The father said he'd sooner see him dead.

We bathed together in the cool water from the jars, we kissed, we wept, and again it was unto death, but this time, already, the pleasure it gave was inconsolable. And then I told him. I told him not to have any regrets, I reminded him of what he'd said, that I'd go away from everywhere, that I wasn't responsible for what I did. He said he didn't mind even that now, nothing counted any more. Then I said I agreed with his father. That I refused to stay with him. I didn't give any reasons.

It's one of the long avenues in Vinh Long that lead down to the Mekong. It's always deserted in the evening. That evening, like most evenings, the electricity breaks down. That's what starts it all off. As soon as I reach the street and the gate shuts behind me, the lights go off. I run. I run because I'm afraid of the dark. I run faster and faster. And suddenly I think I hear running behind me, and suddenly I'm sure that someone's after me. Still running, I look around, and I see. It's a very tall woman, very thin, thin as death, laughing and running. She's barefoot, and she's running after me to catch me. I recognize her, she's the local lunatic, the madwoman of Vinh Long. I hear her for the first time, she talks at night, during the day she sleeps, often here in the avenue, outside the garden. She runs, shouting in a language I don't understand. My fear is so great I can't call out. I must be eight years old. I can hear her shrieks of laughter and cries of delight, she's certainly playing with me. My memory is of a central fear. To say it's beyond my understanding, beyond my strength, is inadequate. What's sure is the memory of my whole being's certainty that if the woman touches me, even lightly, with her hand, I too will enter into a state much worse than death, the state of madness. I manage to get into the neighbors' garden, as far as the house, I run up the steps and fall in the doorway. For several days I can't say anything at all about what happened.

Quite late in life I'm still afraid of seeing a certain state of my mother's—I still don't name it—get so much worse that she'll have to be parted from her children. I believe it will be up to me to recognize the time when it comes, not my brothers, because my brothers wouldn't be able to judge.

It was a few months before our final parting, in Saigon, late one evening, we were on the big terrace of the house in the rue Testard. Dô was there. I looked at my mother, I could hardly recognize her. And then, in a kind of sudden vanishing, a sudden fall, I all at once couldn't recognize her at all. There, suddenly, close to me, was someone sitting in my mother's place who wasn't my mother, who looked like her but who had never been her. She looked rather blank, she was gazing at the garden, a certain point in the garden, it looked as if she was watching for something just about to happen, of which I could see nothing. There was a youthfulness about her features, her expression, a happiness which she was repressing out of what must have been habitual reticence. She was beautiful. Dô was beside her. Dô seemed not to have noticed anything. My terror didn't come from what I've just said about her, her face, her look of happiness, her beauty, it came from the fact that she was sitting just where my mother had been sitting when the substitution took place, from the fact that I knew no one else was there in her place, but that that identity irreplaceable by any other had disappeared and I was powerless to make it come back,

make it start to come back. There was no longer anything there to inhabit her image. I went mad in full
possession of my senses. Just long enough to cry out.
I did cry out. A faint cry, a call for help, to crack the
ice in which the whole scene was fatally freezing. My
mother turned her head.

For me the whole town is inhabited by the beggar
woman in the road. And all the beggar women of the
towns, the rice fields, the tracks bordering Siam, the
banks of the Mekong—for me the beggar woman who
frightened me is inhabited by them. She comes from
everywhere. She always ends up in Calcutta wherever
she started out from. She's always slept in the shade of
the cinnamon-apple trees in the playground. And always my mother has been there beside her, tending
her foot eaten up with maggots and covered with flies.

Beside her, the little girl in the story. She's carried
her two thousand kilometers. She's had enough of her,
wants to give her away. Go on, take her. No more
children. No more child. All dead or thrown away, it
amounts to a lot after a whole life. The one asleep
under the cinnamon-apple trees isn't yet dead. She's
the one who'll live longest. She'll die inside the house,
in a lace dress. She'll be mourned.

She's on the banks of the rice fields on either side
of the track, shouting and laughing at the top of her
voice. She has a golden laugh, fit to wake the dead, to

wake anyone who listens to children's laughter. She stays outside the bungalow for days and days, there are white people in the bungalow, she remembers they give food to beggars. And then one day, lo and behold, she wakes at daybreak and starts to walk, one day she goes, who can tell why, she turns off toward the mountains, goes up through the forest, follows the paths running along the tops of the mountains of Siam. Having seen, perhaps, seen a yellow and green sky on the other side of the plain, she crosses over. At last begins to descend to the sea. With her great gaunt step she descends the slopes of the forest. On, on. They are forests full of pestilence. Regions of great heat. There's no healthy wind from the sea. There's the stagnant din of mosquitoes, dead children, rain every day. And then here are the deltas. The biggest deltas in the world. Made of black slime. Stretching toward Chittagong. She's left the tracks, the forests, the tea roads, the red suns behind, and she goes forward over the estuary of the deltas. She goes in the same direction as the world, toward the engulfing, always distant east. One day she comes face to face with the sea. She lets out a cry, laughs her miraculous birdlike coo. Because of her laugh she finds a junk in Chittagong, the fishermen are willing to take her, she crosses with them the Bay of Bengal.

Then, then she starts to be seen near the rubbish dumps on the outskirts of Calcutta.

And then she's lost sight of. And then later found

again behind the French embassy in the same city. She sleeps in a garden, replete with endless food .

She's there during the night. Then in the Ganges at sunrise. Always laughing, mocking. She doesn't go on this time. Here she can eat, sleep, it's quiet at night, she stays there in the garden with the oleanders.

One day I come, pass by. I'm seventeen. It's the English quarter, the embassy gardens, the monsoon season, the tennis courts are deserted. Along the Ganges the lepers laugh.

We're stopping over in Calcutta. The boat broke down. We're visiting the town to pass the time. We leave the following evening.

Fifteen and a half. The news spreads fast in Sadec. The clothes she wears are enough to show. The mother has no idea, and none about how to bring up a daughter. Poor child. Don't tell me that hat's innocent, or the lipstick, it all means something, it's not innocent, it means something, it's to attract attention, money. The brothers are layabouts. They say it's a Chinese, the son of the millionaire, the villa in Mekong with the blue tiles. And even he, instead of thinking himself honored, doesn't want her for his son. A family of white layabouts.

.   .   .

The Lady, they called her. She came from Savanna Khet. Her husband was posted to Vinh Long. For a year she wasn't seen there. Because of the young man, the assistant administrator in Savanna Khet. They couldn't be lovers any more. So he shot himself. The story reached the new posting in Vinh Long. The day she left Savanna Khet for Vinh Long, a bullet through the heart. In the main square in broad sunlight. Because of her young daughters and her husband's being posted to Vinh Long she'd told him it had to stop.

It goes on in the disreputable quarter of Cholon, every evening. Every morning the little slut goes to have her body caressed by a filthy Chinese millionaire. And she goes to the French high school, too, with the little white girls, the athletic little white girls who learn the crawl in the pool at the Sporting Club. One day they'll be told not to speak to the daughter of the teacher in Sadec any more.

During recess she looks toward the street, all on her own, leaning against a post in the schoolyard. She doesn't say anything about it to her mother. She goes on coming to school in the black limousine belonging to the Chinese in Cholon. She watches it go. No one will break the rule. None of the girls will speak to her. The isolation brings back a clear memory of the lady in Vinh Long. At that time she'd just turned thirty-eight. And the child was ten. And now, when she remembers, she's sixteen.

The lady's on the terrace outside her room, looking at the avenues bordering the Mekong, I see her when I come home from catechism class with my younger brother. The room is in the middle of a great palace with covered terraces, the palace itself in the middle of the garden of oleanders and palms. The same distance separates the lady and the girl in the low-crowned hat from the other people in the town. Just as they both look at the long avenues beside the river, so they are alike in themselves. Both isolated. Alone, queenlike. Their disgrace is a matter of course. Both are doomed to discredit because of the kind of body they have, caressed by lovers, kissed by their lips, consigned to the infamy of a pleasure unto death, as they both call it, unto the mysterious death of lovers without love. That's what it's all about: this hankering for death. It emanates from them, from their rooms, a death so strong its existence is known all over the town, in outposts upcountry, in provincial centers, at official receptions and slow-motion government balls.

The lady has just started giving official receptions again, she thinks it's over, that the young man in Savanna Khet is a thing of the past. So she's started giving evening parties again, the ones expected of her so that people can just meet occasionally and occasionally escape from the frightful loneliness of serving in outposts upcountry, stranded amid checkered stretches of rice, fear, madness, fever, and oblivion.

In the evening, after school, the same black limousine, the same hat at once impudent and childlike, the same lamé shoes, and away she goes, goes to have her body laid bare by the Chinese millionaire, he'll wash her under the shower, slowly, as she used to wash herself at home at her mother's, with cool water from a jar he keeps specially for her, and then he'll carry her, still wet, to the bed, he'll switch on the fan and kiss her more and more all over, and she'll keep asking again and again, and afterwards she'll go back to the boarding school, and no one to punish her, beat her, disfigure or insult her.

It was as night ended that he killed himself, in the main square, glittering with light. She was dancing. Then daylight came, skirted the body. Then, with time, the sunlight blurred its shape. No one dared go near. But the police will. At noon, by the time the tourist boats arrive, there will be nothing left, the square will be empty.

. . .

My mother said to the head of the boarding school, It doesn't matter, all that's of no importance. Haven't you noticed how they suit her, those little old frocks, that pink hat, and the gold shoes? My mother's drunk with delight when she speaks of her children, and that makes her more charming than ever. The young teachers at the boarding school listen to her with passionate attention. All of them, says my mother, they all hang around her, all the men in the place, married or single, they hang around, hanker after the girl, after something not really definite yet, look, she's still a child. Do people talk of disgrace? I say, how can innocence be disgraced?

My mother rattles on. She speaks of blatant prostitution and laughs, at the scandal, the buffoonery, the funny hat, the sublime elegance of the child who crossed the river. And she laughs at what is irresistible here in the French colonies: I mean, she says, this little white tart, this child hidden till then in outposts up-country and suddenly emerging into the daylight and shacking up in front of everyone with this millionaire Chinese scum, with a diamond on her finger just as if she were a banker's wife. And she weeps.

When she saw the diamond she said in a small voice, It reminds me of the little solitaire I had when I got engaged to my first husband. I say: Mr. Dark. We laugh. That was his name, she says, it really was.

We looked at each other for some time, then she gave a sweet, slightly mocking smile, full of so deep a knowledge of her children and what awaited them later on that I almost told her about Cholon.

But I didn't. I never did.

She waited a long while before she spoke again, then she said, very lovingly, You do know it's all over, don't you? That you'll never be able, now, to get married here in the colony? I shrug my shoulders, smile. I say, I can get married anywhere, when I want to. My mother shakes her head. No. She says, Here everything gets known, here you can't, now. She looks at me and says some unforgettable things: They find you attractive? I answer, Yes; they find me attractive in spite of everything. It's then she says, And also because of what you are yourself.

She goes on: Is it only for the money you see him? I hesitate, then say it is only for the money. Again she looks at me for a long while, she doesn't believe me. She says, I wasn't like you, I found school much harder and I was very serious, I stayed like that too long, too late, I lost the taste for my own pleasure.

It was one day during the vacation in Sadec. She was resting in a rocking chair with her feet up on another chair, she'd made a draft between the door of the sitting room and the door of the dining room. She was peaceful, not aggressive. She'd suddenly noticed her daughter, wanted to talk to her.

It happened not long before the end, before she

gave up the land by the dike. Not long before we went back to France.

I watched her fall asleep.

Every so often my mother declares, Tomorrow we'll go to the photographer's. She complains about the price but still goes to the expense of family photos. We look at them, we don't look at each other but we do look at the photographs, each of us separately, without a word of comment, but we look at them, we see ourselves. See the other members of the family one by one or all together. Look back at ourselves when we were very young in the old photos, then look at ourselves again in the recent ones. The gulf between us has grown bigger still. Once they've been looked at the photos are put away with the linen in the closets. My mother has us photographed so that she can see if we're growing normally. She studies us at length, as other mothers do other children. She compares the photos, discusses how each one of us has grown. No one ever answers.

My mother only has photos taken of her children. Never anything else. I don't have any photographs of Vinh Long, not one, of the garden, the river, the straight tamarind-lined avenues of the French conquest, not of the house, nor of our institutional whitewashed bedrooms with the big black-and-gilt iron beds, lit up like classrooms by the red streetlights, the green metal lampshades, not a single image of those incredible places, always temporary, ugly beyond expression, places to flee from, in which my mother would camp until, as she said, she really settled down, but in France, in the regions she's spoken of all her life and that vary, according to her mood, her age, her sadness, between Pas-de-Calais and Entre-Deux-Mers. But when she does halt for good, when she settles down in the Loire, her room will be a terrible replica of the one in Sadec. She will have forgotten.

She never had photos taken of places, of landscapes, only of us, her children, and mostly she had us taken in a group so it wouldn't cost so much. The few amateur photos of us were taken by friends of my mother's, new colleagues just arrived in the colony who took views of the equatorial landscape, the coconut palms, and the coolies to send to their families.

For some mysterious reason my mother used to show her children's photographs to her family when she went home on leave. We didn't want to go and see them. My brothers never met them. At first she used to take me, the youngest, with her. Then later on I stopped going, because my aunts didn't want their daughters to see me any more on account of my shocking behavior. So my mother has only the photographs left to show, so she shows them, naturally, reasonably, shows her cousins her children. She owes it to herself to do so, so she does, her cousins are all that's left of the family, so she shows them the family photos. Can we glimpse something of this woman through this way of going on? The way she sees everything through to the bitter end without ever dreaming she might give up, abandon—the cousins, the effort, the burden. I think we can. It's in this valor, human, absurd, that I see true grace.

When she was old, too, grey-haired, she went to the photographer's, alone, and had her photograph taken in her best dark-red dress and her two bits of jewelry, the locket and the gold and jade brooch, a little round of jade sheathed in gold. In the photo her hair is done nicely, her clothes just so, butter wouldn't melt in her mouth. The better-off natives used to go to the photographer's too, just once in their lives, when they saw death was near. Their photos were large, all the same size, hung in handsome gilt frames near the altars to their ancestors. All these photographs of different people, and I've seen many of them, gave practically identical results, the resemblance was stunning. It wasn't just because all old people look alike, but because the portraits themselves were invariably touched up in such a way that any facial peculiarities, if there were any left, were minimized. All the faces were prepared in the same way to confront eternity, all toned down, all uniformly rejuvenated. This was what people wanted. This general resemblance, this tact, would characterize the memory of their passage through the family, bear witness at once to the singularity and to the reality of that transit. The more they resembled each other the more evidently they belonged in the ranks of the family. Moreover, all the men wore the same sort of turban, all the women had their hair scraped back into the same kind of bun, and both men and women wore tunics with stand-up collars. And they all wore an expression I'd still recognize anywhere. My mother's expression in the photograph with the red dress was the same. Noble, some would say. Others would call it withdrawn.

They never speak of it any more. It's an understood thing that he won't approach his father any more to let him marry her. That the father will have no pity on his son. He has no pity on anyone. Of all the Chinese immigrants who hold the trade of the place in their hands, the man with the blue terraces is the most terrible, the richest, the one whose property extends the farthest beyond Sadec, to Cholon, the Chinese capital of French Indochina. The man from Cholon knows his father's decision and the girl's are the same, and both are irrevocable. To a lesser degree he begins to understand that the journey which will separate him from her is a piece of good luck for their affair. That she's not the marrying kind, she'll run away from any marriage, he must give her up, forget her, give her back to the whites, to her brothers.

Ever since he'd been infatuated with her body the girl had stopped being incommoded by it, by its thinness. And similarly, strangely, her mother no longer worried about it as she had before, just as if she too had discovered it was plausible after all, as acceptable as any other body. The lover from Cholon thinks the growth of the little white girl has been stunted by the excessive heat. He too was born and grew up in this heat. He discovers this kinship between them. He says all the years she's spent here, in this intolerable latitude, have turned her into a girl of Indochina. That she has the same slender wrists as they, the same thick hair that looks as if it's absorbed all its owner's strength, and it's long like theirs too, and above all there's her skin, all over her body, that comes from the rainwater stored here for women and children to bathe in. He says compared with the women here the women in France have hard skins on their bodies, almost rough. He says the low diet of the tropics, mostly fish and fruit, has something to do with it too. Also the cottons and silks the clothes here are made of, and the loose clothes themselves, leaving a space between themselves and the body, leaving it naked, free.

The lover from Cholon is so accustomed to the adolescence of the white girl, he's lost. The pleasure he takes in her every evening has absorbed all his time, all his life. He scarcely speaks to her any more. Perhaps he thinks she won't understand any longer what he'd say about her, about the love he never knew before and of which he can't speak. Perhaps he realizes they never have spoken to each other, except when they cry out to each other in the bedroom in the evening. Yes, I think he didn't know, he realizes he didn't know.

He looks at her. Goes on looking at her, his eyes shut. He inhales her face, breathes it in. He breathes her in, the child, his eyes shut he breathes in her breath, the warm air coming out of her. Less and less clearly can he make out the limits of this body, it's not like other bodies, it's not finished, in the room it keeps growing, it's still without set form, continually coming into being, not only there where it's visible but elsewhere too, stretching beyond sight, toward risk, toward death, it's nimble, it launches itself wholly into pleasure as if it were grown up, adult, it's without guile, and it's frighteningly intelligent.

. . .

I used to watch what he did with me, how he used me, and I'd never thought anyone could act like that, he acted beyond my hope and in accordance with my body's destiny. So I became his child. And he became something else for me too. I began to recognize the inexpressible softness of his skin, of his member, apart from himself. The shadow of another man must have passed through the room, the shadow of a young murderer, but I didn't know that then, had no inkling of it yet. The shadow of a young hunter must have passed through the room too, but that one, yes, I knew about, sometimes he was present in the pleasure and I'd tell the lover from Cholon, talk to him of the other's body and member, of his indescribable sweetness, of his courage in the forest and on the rivers whose estuaries hold the black panthers. Everything chimed with his desire and made him possess me. I had become his child. It was with his own child he made love every evening. And sometimes he takes fright, suddenly he's worried about her health, as if he suddenly realized she was mortal and it suddenly struck him he might lose her. Her being so thin strikes him, and sometimes this makes him suddenly afraid. And there's the headache, too, which often makes her lie limp, motionless, ghastly pale, with a wet bandage over her eyes. And the loathing of life that sometimes seizes her, when she thinks of her mother and suddenly cries out and weeps with rage at the thought of not being able to change things, not being able to make her mother happy before she dies, not being able to kill those responsible. His face against hers he receives her tears, crushes her to him, mad with desire for her tears, for her anger.

He takes her as he would his own child. He'd take his own child the same way. He plays with his child's body, turns it over, covers his face with it, his lips, his eyes. And she, she goes on abandoning herself in exactly the same way as he set when he started. Then suddenly it's she who's imploring, she doesn't say what for, and he, he shouts to her to be quiet, that he doesn't want to have anything more to do with her, doesn't want to have his pleasure of her any more. And now once more they are caught together, locked together in terror, and now the terror abates again, and now they succumb to it again, amid tears, despair, and happiness.

They are silent all evening long. In the black car that takes her back to the boarding school she leans her head on his shoulder. He puts his arm around her. He says it's a good thing the boat from France is coming soon to take her away and separate them. They are silent during the drive. Sometimes he tells the driver to go around by the river. She sleeps, exhausted, on his shoulder. He wakes her with kisses.

In the dormitory the light is blue. There's a smell of incense, they always burn incense at dusk. The heat is oppressive, all the windows are wide open, and there's not a breath of air. I take my shoes off so as not to make any noise, but I'm not worried, I know the mistress in charge won't get up, I know it's accepted now that I come back at night at whatever time I like. I go straight to where H.L. is, always slightly anxious, always afraid she may have run away during the day. But she's there. She sleeps deeply, H.L. An obstinate, almost hostile sleep, I remember. Expressing rejection. Her bare arms are flung up in abandon around her head. Her body is not lying down decorously like those of the other girls, her legs are bent, her face is invisible, her pillow awry. I expect she was waiting for me but fell asleep as she waited, impatient and angry. She must have been crying too, and then lapsed into oblivion. I'd like to wake her up, have a whispered conversation. I don't talk to the man from Cholon any more, he doesn't talk to me, I need to hear H.L.'s questions. She has the matchless attentiveness of those who don't understand what is said to them. But I can't wake her up. Once she's awakened like that, in the middle of the night, H.L. can't go back to sleep again. She gets up, wants to go outside, does so, goes down the stairs, along the corridors, out all alone into the big empty playgrounds, she runs, she calls out to me, she's so happy, it's irresistible, and when she's not allowed to go out with the other girls, you know that's just what she wants. I hesitate, but then no, I don't wake her up. Under the mosquito net the heat is stifling, when you close the net after you it seems unendurable. But I know it's because I've come in from outside, from the banks of the river where it's always cool at night. I'm used to it, I keep still, wait for it to pass. It passes. I never fall asleep right away despite the new fatigues in my life. I think about the man from Cholon. He's probably in a nightclub somewhere near the Fountain with his driver, they'll be drinking in silence, they drink arrack when they're on their own. Or else he's gone home, he's fallen asleep with the light on, still without speaking to anyone. That night I can't bear the thought of the man from Cholon any more. Nor the thought of H.L. It's as if they were happy, and as if it came from outside themselves. And I have nothing like that. My mother says, This one will never be satisfied with anything. I think I'm beginning to see my life. I think I can already say, I have a vague desire to die. From now on I treat that word and my life as inseparable. I think I have a vague desire to be alone, just as I realize I've never been alone any more since I left childhood behind, and the family of the hunter. I'm going to write.

That's what I see beyond the present moment, in the great desert in whose form my life stretches out before me.

I forget the words of the telegram from Saigon. Forget whether it said my younger brother was dead or whether it said, Recalled to God. I seem to remember it was Recalled to God. I realized at once, she couldn't have sent the telegram. My younger brother. Dead. At first it's incomprehensible, and then suddenly, from all directions, from the ends of the earth, comes pain. It buried me, swept me away, I didn't know anything, I ceased to exist except for pain, what pain, I didn't know what pain, whether it was the pain returning of having lost a child a few months before, or a new pain. Now I think it was a new pain, I'd never known my still-born child and hadn't wanted to kill myself then as I wanted to now.

It was a mistake, and that momentary error filled the universe. The outrage was on the scale of God. My younger brother was immortal and they hadn't noticed. Immortality had been concealed in my brother's body while he was alive, and we hadn't noticed that it dwelt there. Now my brother's body was dead, and immortality with it. And the world went on without that visited body, and without its visitation. It was a complete mistake. And the error, the outrage, filled the whole universe.

. . .

Since my younger brother was dead, everything had
to die after him. And through him. Death, a chain
reaction of death, started with him, the child.

The corpse of the child was unaffected, itself, by the
events of which it was the cause. Of the immortality
it had harbored for the twenty-seven years of its life,
it didn't know the name.

No one saw clearly but I. And since I'd acquired that
knowledge, the simple knowledge that my younger
brother's body was mine as well, I had to die. And I
am dead. My younger brother gathered me to him,
drew me to him, and I am dead.

People ought to be told of such things. Ought to be
taught that immortality is mortal, that it can die, it's
happened before and it happens still. It doesn't ever
announce itself as such—it's duplicity itself. It doesn't
exist in detail, only in principle. Certain people may
harbor it, on condition they don't know that's what
they're doing. Just as certain other people may detect
its presence in them, on the same condition, that they
don't know they can. It's while it's being lived that life
is immortal, while it's still alive. Immortality is not a
matter of more or less time, it's not really a question of

immortality but of something else that remains unknown. It's as untrue to say it's without beginning or
end as to say it begins and ends with the life of the
spirit, since it partakes both of the spirit and of the
pursuit of the void. Look at the dead sands of the
desert, the dead bodies of children: there's no path for
immortality there, it must halt and seek another way.

In the case of my younger brother it was an immortality
without flaw, without commentary, smooth, pure,
unique. My younger brother had nothing to cry in the
wilderness, he had nothing to say, here or anywhere,
nothing. He was uneducated, he never managed to
learn anything. He couldn't speak, could scarcely read,
scarcely write, sometimes you'd think he couldn't even
suffer. He was someone who didn't understand and was
afraid.

The wild love I feel for him remains an unfathomable
mystery to me. I don't know why I loved him so much
as to want to die of his death. I'd been parted from him
for ten years when it happened, and hardly ever thought
about him. I loved him, it seemed, forever, and nothing
new could happen to that love. I'd forgotten about
death.

. . .

We didn't talk to each other much, we hardly talked at all about our elder brother, or our unhappiness, our mother's unhappiness, the misfortune of the land on the plain. We talked instead about hunting, rifles, mechanics, cars. He'd get furious about our worn-down old car and tell me about, describe, the cars he'd have in the future. I knew all the makes of hunting rifles and all the brands of cars. We also talked, of course, about being eaten by tigers if we weren't careful, or getting drowned in the river if we went on swimming in the currents. He was two years older than I.

The wind has ceased, and under the trees there's the supernatural light that follows rain. Some birds are shrieking at the tops of their voices, crazy birds. As they sharpen their beaks on it, the cold air rings with an almost deafening clamor.

The liners used to go up the Saigon River, engines off, drawn by tugs to the port installations in the bend of the Mekong that's on the same latitude as the town of Saigon. This bend or branch of the Mekong is called the River, the Saigon River. The boats stopped there for a week. As soon as they berthed, you were in France. You could dine in France and dance there, but it was too expensive for my mother, and anyway for her there was no point. But with him, the lover from Cholon, you could have gone. But he didn't go because he'd have been afraid to be seen with the little white girl, so young. He didn't say, but she knew. In those days, and it's not so long ago, scarcely fifty years, it was only ships that went all over the world. Large parts of all the continents were still without roads or railways. Hundreds, thousands of square kilometers still had nothing but prehistoric tracks. It was the handsome ships of the Messageries Maritimes, the musketeers of the shipping lines, the Porthos, D'Artagnan, and Aramis, that linked Indochina to France.

The voyage lasted twenty-four days. The liners were like towns, with streets, bars, cafés, libraries, drawing rooms, meetings, lovers, weddings, deaths. Chance societies formed, fortuitous as everyone knew and did not forget, but for that very reason tolerable, and sometimes unforgettably pleasant. These were the only voyages the women ever made. And for many of them, and for some men too, the voyage out to the colony was the real adventure of the whole thing. For our mother those trips, together with our infancy, were always what she called "the happiest days of her life."

Departures. They were always the same. Always the first departures over the sea. People have always left the land in the same sorrow and despair, but that never stopped men from going, Jews, philosophers, and pure travelers for the journey's own sake. Nor did it ever stop women letting them go, the women who never went themselves, who stayed behind to look after the birthplace, the race, the property, the reason for the return. For centuries, because of the ships, journeys were longer and more tragic than they are today. A voyage covered its distance in a natural span of time. People were used to those slow human speeds on both land and sea, to those delays, those waitings on the wind or fair weather, to those expectations of shipwreck, sun, and death. The liners the little white girl knew were among the last mailboats in the world. It was while she was young that the first airlines were started, which were gradually to deprive mankind of journeys across the sea.

We still went every day to the flat in Cholon. He behaved as usual, for a while he behaved as usual, giving me a shower with the water from the jars, carrying me over to the bed. He'd come over to me, lie down too, but now he had no strength, no potency. Once the date of my departure was fixed, distant thought it still was, he could do nothing with my body any more. It had happened suddenly, without his realizing it. His body wanted nothing more to do with the body that was about to go away, to betray. He'd say, I can't make love to you any more, I thought I still could, but I can't. He'd say he was dead. He'd give a sweet, apologetic smile, say that perhaps it would never come back. I'd ask him if that's what he wanted. He, almost laughing, would say, I don't know, at this moment perhaps yes. His gentleness was unaffected by his pain. He didn't speak of the pain, never said a word about it. Sometimes his face would quiver, he'd close his eyes and clench his teeth. But he never said anything about the images he saw behind his closed eyes. It was as if he loved the pain, loved it as he'd loved me, intensely, unto death perhaps, and as if he preferred it now to me. Sometimes he'd say he'd like to caress me because he knew I longed for it, and he'd like to watch me as the pleasure came. So he did, and watched me at the same time, and called me his child. We decided not to see each other any more, but it wasn't possible, it turned out to be impossible. Every evening he was there outside the high school in his black car, his head averted from humiliation.

When it was due to sail the boat gave three blasts on its siren, very long and terribly loud, they were heard all over the town, and over the harbor the sky grew dark. Then the tugs came up and towed the boat to the middle of the river, after which they cast off their cables and returned to harbor. Then the boat bade farewell again, uttering once more its terrible, mysteriously sad wails that made everyone weep, not only those who were parting from one another but the onlookers too, and those who were there for no special reason, who had no one particular in mind. Then, very slowly, under its own steam, the boat launched itself on the river. For a long while its tall shape could be seen advancing toward the sea. Many people stayed to watch, waving more and more slowly, more and more sadly, with scarves and handkerchiefs. Then finally the outline of the ship was swallowed up in the curve of the earth. On a clear day you could see it slowly sink.

For her too it was when the boat uttered its first farewell, when the gangway was hauled up and the tugs had started to tow and draw the boat away from land, that she had wept. She'd wept without letting anyone see her tears, because he was Chinese and one oughtn't to weep for that kind of lover. Wept without letting her mother or her younger brother see she was sad, without letting them see anything, as was the custom between them. His big car was there, long and black with the white-liveried driver in front. It was a little way away from the Messageries Maritimes car park, on its own. That was how she'd recognized it. That was him in the back, that scarcely visible shape, motionless, overcome. She was leaning on the rails, like the first time, on the ferry. She knew he was watching her. She was watching him too, she couldn't see him any more but she still looked toward the shape of the black car. And then at last she couldn't see it any more. The harbor faded away, and then the land.

There was the China Sea, the Red Sea, the Indian Ocean, the Suez Canal, the morning when you woke up and knew from the absence of vibration that you were advancing through the sand. But above all there was the ocean. The furthest, the most vast, it reached to the South Pole. It had the longest distance between landfalls, between Ceylon and Somalia. Sometimes it was so calm, and the weather so fair and mild, that crossing it was like a journey over something other than the sea. Then the whole boat opened up, the lounges, the gangways, the portholes, and the passengers fled their sweltering cabins and slept on deck.

Once, during the crossing of the ocean, late at night, someone died. She can't quite remember if it was on that voyage or another that it happened. Some people were playing cards in the first-class bar, and among the players was a young man who at one point, without saying anything, laid down his cards, left the bar, ran across the deck, and threw himself into the sea. By the time the boat was stopped—it was going at full speed —the body couldn't be found.

No, now she comes to write it down she doesn't see the boat, but somewhere else, the place where she was told about it. It was in Sadec. It was the son of the district officer in Sadec. She knew him, he'd been at the high school in Saigon too. She remembers him, dark, tall, with a very gentle face and horn-rimmed glasses. Nothing was found in his cabin, no farewell letter. His age has remained in her memory, terrifying, the same, seventeen. The boat went on again at dawn. That was the worst. The sunrise, the empty sea, and the decision to abandon the search. The parting.

And another time, on the same route, during the crossing of the same ocean, night had begun as before and in the lounge on the main deck there was a sudden burst of music, a Chopin waltz which she knew secretly, personally, because for months she had tried to learn it, though she never managed to play it properly, never, and that was why her mother agreed to let her give up the piano. Among all the other nights upon nights, the girl had spent that one on the boat, of that she was sure, and she'd been there when it happened, the burst of Chopin under a sky lit up with brilliancies. There wasn't a breath of wind and the music spread all over the dark boat, like a heavenly injunction whose import was unknown, like an order from God whose meaning was inscrutable. And the girl started up as if to go and kill herself in her turn, throw herself in her turn into the sea, and afterwards she wept because she thought of the man from Cholon and suddenly she wasn't sure she hadn't loved him with a love she hadn't seen because it had lost itself in the affair like water in sand and she rediscovered it only now, through this moment of music flung across the sea.

As later she had seen the eternity of her younger brother, through death.

Around her, people slept, enveloped but not awakened by the music, peaceful. The girl thought she'd just seen the calmest night there had ever been in the Indian Ocean. She thinks it's during that night too that she saw her younger brother come on deck with a woman. He leaned on the rails, she put her arms around him, and they kissed. The girl hid to get a better view. She recognized the woman. Already, with her younger brother, the two were always together. She was a married woman, but it was a dead couple, the husband appeared not to notice anything. During the last few days of the voyage the younger brother and the woman spent all day in their cabin, they came out only at night. During these same days the younger brother looked at his mother and sister as if he didn't know them. The mother grew grim, silent, jealous. She, the girl, wept. She was happy, she thought, and at the same time she was afraid of what would happen later to her younger brother. She thought he'd leave them, go off with the woman, but no, he came back to them when they got to France.

She doesn't know how long it was after the white girl left that he obeyed his father's orders, married as he was told to do the girl the families had chosen ten years ago, a girl dripping, like the rest, with gold, diamonds, jade. She too was a Chinese from the north, from the city of Fushun, and had come there with relations.

It must have been a long time before he was able to be with her, to give her the heir to their fortunes. The memory of the little white girl must have been there, lying there, the body, across the bed. For a long time she must have remained the queen of his desire, his personal link with emotion, with the immensity of tenderness, the dark and terrible depths of the flesh. Then the day must have come when it was possible. The day when desire for the little white girl was so strong, so unbearable that he could find her whole image again as in a great and raging fever, and pene-trate the other woman with his desire for her, the white child. Through a lie he must have found himself inside the other woman, through a lie providing what their families, Heaven, and the northern ancestors expected of him, to wit, an heir to their name.

Perhaps she knew about the white girl. She had native servants in Sadec who knew about the affair and must have talked. She couldn't not have known of his sorrow. They must both have been the same age, sixteen. That night, had she seen her husband weep? And, seeing it, had she offered consolation? A girl of sixteen, a Chinese fiancée of the thirties, could she without impropriety offer consolation for such an adulterous sorrow at her expense? Who knows? Perhaps she was mistaken, perhaps the other girl wept with him, not speaking for the rest of the night. And then love might have come after, after the tears.

But she, the white girl, never knew anything of all this.

Years after the war, after marriages, children, divorces, books, he came to Paris with his wife. He phoned her. It's me. She recognized him at once from the voice. He said, I just wanted to hear your voice. She said, It's me, hello. He was nervous, afraid, as before. His voice suddenly trembled. And with the trembling, suddenly,

she heard again the voice of China. He knew she'd
begun writing books, he'd heard about it through her
mother whom he'd met again in Saigon. And about
her younger brother, and he'd been grieved for her.
Then he didn't know what to say. And then he told
her. Told her that it was as before, that he still loved
her, he could never stop loving her, that he'd love her
until death.

Neauphle-le-Château–Paris
February–May 1984